SYNTHEDROID SAVIORS

MARK LINDQUIST

LINK BRANCH PRESS

LINK BRANCH PRESS

For information on book sales contact:
Link Branch Press
P.O. Box 1762
Warren, Michigan 48090
e-mail: etimespace@sbcglobal.net

Find forthcoming Web site by Internet search for— Link Branch Press

FIRST EDITION 2007

Computer graphics by Drago Domazet

Author photo by Petru Mihali

Library of Congress Control Number: 2007932872

ISBN: 978-0-9798202-0-5

10 9 8 7 6 5 4 3 2 1

Printed in the United States of America

CONTENTS

AUTHOR'S PREFACE

I began to write this work with the intention of creating quality science fiction, which, unfortunately, is quite rare. Sadly, the Earth may soon reclaim sci-fi master Arthur C. Clarke (90 in 2007). I ride his tsunami of karmic momentum with many other writers.

As *Synthedroid Saviors* evolved, my knowledge of Eastern thought (predominantly Zen Buddhism) launched it into an unknown genre. Through the writing process, I realized a path toward ontological invention, creative critiquing, tricksterism, and striking satisfaction. The first draft was completed in August 2006.

The underground nature of this novel will aid the "dinner party" revolution I envision in the early twenty-first century. The party in mind is one of reason, debate, and intuition rather than bloodshed. I playfully ponder that Gandhi, Alan Watts, Marx (Groucho, Woodo, Karlo?), and Kurt Vonnegut reflect my thinking and would have approved this brand of partying. Please read the book with careful inquiry and judge for yourself.

No dedication page is necessary—just the names above.

Mark Lindquist
Space-time Continuum
July 2007

The working title of my second novel is *Mutinous Mothers.* The sequel to *Synthedroid Saviors* non-exists in ideation.

PRELUDE

On a flight back to the States, Phil woke from a nap. He had just dreamed that the synthedroids discovered an antipodal cosmos where reincarnated insects founded a church. Phil was journeying there to condemn bug theology as the nightmare ended.

After the last flight segment, Phil began to jog the twelve kilometers back home. It was Halloween and he saw children wearing screen masks. The screen mask could project any face on its surface. Some transmitted Madam President or various celebrities; others depicted synthedroid faces. Phil stopped when his own face appeared. While he stared at the kid inches from the mask, the accompanying parents smiled and asked for his autograph. The handwritten name was given during a bit of friendly chatter.

Phil finally arrived home, took a shower, and checked the Internet for recent news. A story came up about Tria receiving criticism while lecturing. Her pontificating, including the declaration that a new calendar should be adopted to reset 2031 to year one, irritated the crowd. The reporter printed the end of Tria's speech as her response.

She stated, "It's stunning to realize that–throughout history–every philosopher, scientist, theist, and metaphysicist got it wrong to some degree. I may be just another voice in a long line of failures. This is the ultimate cosmic joke. Don't believe me—make a diligent, objective search for yourself."

Phil smiled at Tria's dedication to truthfulness.

Moving to another article, an account of a senior monk at a Zen monastery revealed the difficulty of training. The teacher, an elderly Zen master, was near death and the monk demanded to know the ultimate reality. The old master told him that the wind whipping the grass held this truth. He discussed this answer and its possible implications with the other monks. One monk, a novice who had just arrived at the monastery, asked what this nonsense phrase meant. The senior monk went back to the Zen master to clear up the confusion.

The monk asked, "What does the wind whipping the grass represent?"

The master said, "It represents the water dripping from the sky."

The monk asked, "What does that mean?"

The master shouted, "Okay, it doesn't mean anything. I come from a long tradition of liars!"

Phil moved onto an intriguing story. It was amusing, yet heartbreaking. Gorillas had become extinct in the wild in 2028. Gorillas in captivity diminished—somehow, they knew their fate and were resigned to the lack of a breeding population. Newborns died despite all human efforts; the last one had expired a week earlier.

Okok, the last living gorilla, had a sign language vocabulary of fifteen hundred words and could understand more than two thousand English words. She had a definite resemblance to Gerry Rabidson. In an interview, Okok was asked if she believed in God. This final member of a doomed species pondered the question carefully.

Then Okok signed the answer. "There is no gorilla god."

CHAPTER 1—ANTHROPIVOTAL

Dr. Ping Chou and Master Wu Li made several attempts to create another synthetic mind. All efforts had failed to produce a living, unified web of neurons that had been achieved with SYNA (Synthetic Yinyang Neuron Actuated). The two women received widely varying analyses on their unsuccessful efforts to reproduce the miracle of this first brain without a body. The most likely reason for their inability to realize the same result was that the critical phase of development in the fetus brain, which had become SYNA, occurred during a freak anomaly. The brain had been removed from its body at the first and pivotal stage when it could survive separation. This was the precise moment when neuron stem cell activity had climaxed. This giant-leap-for-humankind surgery took place on a day when the largest solar flare in recorded history had temporarily reversed the polarity of Earth's electromagnetic field. The effect of this created strange behavior in some animals. Numerous bird flocks that normally flew north that day were flying south. Dolphins in captivity emitted sounds never heard before. The electromagnetic state of the Earth on that day could not be completely quantified or qualified.

Because of this quirk of conditions, Wu Li and Ping were able to nurture this neural plexus over a six-month period until it had grown to more than ten times the size of an adult brain—fifteen kilos. Visually, it did not resemble a human brain. When given free space to grow in a unique amniotic-like fluid, it began a life of its own.

Did SYNA have an independent consciousness? It was all very uncertain in the first days and months of the Link. The world network organization known as the Link came into being to guide the experiences of the synthenauts. Synthenaut was the name given to humans that connected their minds to SYNA through the 4D chip link.

In 2026 a new eon began. Human chip implant engineering stepped from prototype into production. It was a time of transformation of life that revealed a self-created spiritual revolution.

The Link joined universities and research groups around the spheroid via Internet and Cybernet. They were technicians, scientists, and the elite circle of synthenauts.

On a luminous spring morning, representatives of Link Nodes gathered near the mobile sculpture in front of the United Nations Building. They walked to an informal convention in Central Park. Members looked up and marveled at the recently finished Geodesic Polydome that completely covered Manhattan.

The Polydome was constructed with struts composed of an alloy that contained titanium and buckytube carbon—these formed the skeleton. The skin, an artificial glass membrane, blocked most ultraviolet radiation and generated electricity by converting the heat energy it absorbed. Polydome filters removed impurities from the air; internal combustion engines were banned on Manhattan.

The island's even numbered streets were designated for electric vehicles and odd streets flowed with bicycle traffic. Link representatives crossed intersections that seemed like part of a twentieth century Chinese city with the never-ending stream of bicycles. Ambient vibes in the air made the members somewhat light-hearted and celebratory. When arriving at the site near the Strawberry Fields Memorial, they sat on the grass. Lilacs perfumed the air.

There were various small groups, either supporting or protesting, around the periphery. A member of one faction with a long beard and robe stood perfectly still. His hands were raised in the air as if to send blessings or receive vibratory energy. A dog had mistaken him for a tree and urinated on his feet. Other gaggles held demonstration signs with phrases like: "No brains in a box" (referring to SYNA), "Satan was a stem cell engineer," and "Don't add to nature's freak show."

The business of this casual convention primarily involved electing a chairperson to lead the Link. In the front near the stage were the candidates. They represented Beijing Node, MIT, Cambridge University, Mecca Node, Vatican Node, and Bangkok University.

After a divided first vote, leading members of the Link began to make statements. The ageing, small-framed Patpong Chuen, a saffron-robed monk from Bangkok University, was first to speak.

He declared, "It is clear that the Chiists (pronounced Chee-ists) and Chippists are evenly divided. The commonplace, gregarious activities of this mundane gathering in the greenery of New York does not compare in any way to the conflicting experiences of synthenauts. Our disagreements are centered on the 4D chip created for link-up with SYNA, the synthetic mind. Does the 4D chip enable us to communicate with SYNA and does it possibly enable a transcendence of space-time? It seems to come to this simple question.

"The Chiists believe freedom from space-time can be realized only in one's own mind through intensive meditation. My faction, the Chippists, believes this freedom comes through the 4D chip link to SYNA. I have been a lifetime meditator and, at eighty-three years old, am the oldest human to have a 4D chip implant with a link to my mirror neuron network. At least most of us agree that these experiences cannot be put into words; however, words are all I can offer in this moment.

"One point of debate I will take a side on is the question of whether SYNA is an independent mind or new life form. Yes is my answer, but how do I define life? My definition is this: life is, conventionally, something that has genetic structure and can replicate itself. Also, with development, life is a consciousness that understands the meaning and dynamics of happiness/suffering, pleasure/pain, form/space—dualistic reality. SYNA has demonstrated the latter—a kind of consciousness I experienced through the 4D chip link. These link-up encounters are, ironically, outside of dualistic space-time so we must depend on deeper insight.

"We are all aware of the recent uproar by conservative religious organizations at this proclamation of human-designed life. One extremist group staged a funeral for embryonic stem cells that had been altered by the Link. I found it unbelievable that several indoctrinated members of this group needed grief counseling after the service. We have all personally endured insults and attacks from these types of pitiful, head-shrunken fanatics. Most of us agree, though, that the Link has momentum and cannot be stopped. We will be a quantum surge of spirituality that leaves past and present theologies in the same place as sticks used by chimps to extract insects. With this thought in mind, I will turn over the podium to Cardinal Poltramck of the Vatican Node."

The audience clapped, cheered, and laughed. Patpong Chuen bowed to the introduced speaker as he walked off the stage.

Dressed casually, the Cardinal stepped to the microphone and began. "My stick has developed substantially since my distant relative with the hairy buttocks. At least I didn't wear outrageous religious headgear on stage (more laughter). Well, as many of you know my position as a Chiist differs from Dr. Chuen's even though we agree the SYNA experience has dimensions of pleasure and pain along with the desire of happiness over suffering. Since I was selected to undergo the 4D chip link implant, I joined an elite group of about one hundred men and women from around the planetoid who have come in contact with SYNA. My experience was that this synthetic brain is only conscious when linked to synthenauts and is, in reality, an extension of our own mind. SYNA, when disconnected, is merely electrical pulses and neurochemical transmissions circulating in a system of synthetic neurons with their endless labyrinth of axons and dendrites. The spirit is in synthenaut humankind and not in synthetic neuron constructions. This synthetic mind only has human sensitivities when linked with synthenauts. I believe that, on its own, autonomous consciousness and spirit do not exist. Of course, this is a mystery and will be constantly debated until, if possible, SYNA can speak independently. Even if we had a speaking entity, we will not all agree that this is a completely unaided mind.

"Well, our time is limited and we agreed to be short winded. Let me introduce our next speaker—Dr. Noor Amrak of the Mecca Node."

Applause sounded as Cardinal Poltramck left the stage. He nodded to Noor.

Dr. Amrak confidently approached the lectern and began. "I thank you Cardinal Poltramck. Looking back to the Cardinal's first comment involving a hairy male buttocks, I realized that women have made greater evolutionary advances."

She turned away from the assemblage, bent over, and dropped her pants to the knees exposing her rear end. Then she quickly pulled them up and returned to the lectern. Noor was met with roaring revelry.

She continued, "Yes, a hairless female buttocks is proof of an advanced life form. Not too many years ago, as an Islamic woman, I could have been put to death for that display. Thankfully, we are moving away from the Achilles heel of Islam—female subservience.

"To get on with the subject at hand, I will speak of my experience as a synthenaut and my contribution as a result of that experience. I too agree, the synthetic brain seems to have human understanding, but like Cardinal Poltramck, I am not sure where my mind ends and SYNA's starts. It is a realization that mind is solitary, yet connected with all minds–a paradox that can only be known by being a synthenaut.

"This brings me to my contribution involving Islamic thought, which I discuss at length in my book disc—here I will only touch on it briefly. Being a synthenaut has aided me in going beyond relative, dualistic space-time while in meditation. This state of mind has revealed true nature and has made me aware of various false images of God. God is non-dualistic, non-conceptual Absolute–not restricted by our relative, dualistic space-time. Beyond conception and definition there is no possible image or personification for God. Perhaps Muslims are a bit ahead of Christians and Hindus in that we have no likeness or physical image for God. Any attempt to have a conception of God is relative, where one object or concept is thought of in dualistic reference to other objects or concepts. This thinking and indeed all thinking have no place in the non-conceptual Absolute—the realm of God. I am grateful that so many worldwide are beginning to see this. Some of my Buddhist colleagues agree this is a positive step in Western religious understanding.

"Getting back to the major division in this group assembled today, I like the Cardinal, am a Chiist. I believe any true spiritual experience is within one's own mind. Buddhists and Hindus have held this as truth centuries before Christians and Muslims existed. Most of us are surprised, though, at the slight irony of so many Buddhist members of the Link being Chippists. Regardless of that, I can only speak from my own understanding. SYNA is a very seductive friend, but I believe this 'friend' is only an extension of our mind.

"Because of this, I give my support to the largest Chiist faction vote receiver—Master Wu Li of the Beijing Node."

Dr. Amrak finished abruptly, walked off stage up to the front row, and took the arm of the Maha Lama. As she walked him to the microphone, cotton-like clouds moved slowly off to the horizon exhibiting the Polydome's triangular patchwork of shadows on the grass. Just as the Maha Lama reached center stage, the sun opened up on him as he smiled and greeted the audience with hands together at chest height.

The Maha Lama began. "Even a ninety year old monk can appreciate the artistic curves of Dr. Amrak's buttocks."

The assembly offered some polite laughter.

He continued, "As many of you have heard, I was denied the privilege of having a 4D chip link implanted because of my health and age. However, the encounter with synthenauts I have counseled has revealed to me that SYNA is not a connection or extension of mind, but a human-developed and reasoning life form. Other synthenauts disagree, but my detailed conversations with Buddhist monk synthenauts have convinced me to become part of the Chippist faction.

"Not since the time of the Siddhartha Gautama, the Buddha, has there been such a revolution in human spirituality. We, I believe, have melded our minds with our own creation. The Buddha himself would have been dumbfounded by these recent revelations. I hope in coming weeks and months those of all faiths and philosophies will follow the development of the Link and judge for themselves the new reality of our age.

"Well, I have made the crucial points of my position on the Link's direction. I just wanted to finish by quelling the rumor that I levitated from the airport to Central Park. My levitation was restricted to the sudden drop on my flight during a thunderstorm."

Again, there was a polite cheerful reaction.

"So who is our next speaker?"

Technicians pointed to a monitor on the left side of the stage. After clearing his throat, the Maha Lama recognized the name and sighed warmly.

He exclaimed, "Ah, Phil Ubique, I have not seen you since you visited me at the Potala. Please come up; I am curious at what your latest data shows on this world-shaking project."

Again, Dr. Noor Amrak assisted the Maha Lama. As they left the stage, he gently patted her butt, which was responded to by cheers and shouts.

As Dr. Ubique came to the steps, he joyfully greeted the Maha Lama and whispered in his ear, "At your age, you can get away with more than me." Then Phil turned to Noor and said, "May I touch it?" pointing downward.

She replied, "If I were not married, you might have had a chance."

With a smile, she walked away arm in arm with the Lama.

Dr. Ubique stepped up to the microphone, checked his chronometer and began. "Moving from the quantifiable nanotechnology to unquantifiable Link technology, we break with all human history and enter a new reality. In the next twenty years, the Link will bring the 4D chip link to anyone who desires to be transfigured. The cost of the technology will be negligible given a little more time for research and development.

"At this point among the synthenauts, I have logged the most hours linked to SYNA. I helped innovate the surgical technique for implanting 4D chips and link-up connectors in the labs at MIT. In the last year, the implanted 4D chips have been refined and are now considered safe for most to have this augmentation realized. Among the hundred men and women selected for an implant, none have had any medical abnormalities directly related to the 4D chip. In a few synthenauts, former medical and psychological problems have flared up—like the unfortunate Sylvia Tiltohinn whose kleptomania condition recurred recently. After careful investigation, though, it was determined that Tiltohinn's thieving tendencies had no connection to implants.

"Much has happened since the genesis of the first synthetic mind in the laboratory of Dr. Ping Chou and Master Wu Li. Even though SYNA lacks conventional cells and bodily processes, it is still the first formulated synthetic humanoid mind. In the first 4D chip link to SYNA, my experience was like having a child asking questions and me responding intuitively. Later, this developed into a conversation with no one speaking and with no sense of time or space. Many of the synthenauts have had this apparent mutual acquaintance.

"I remember when I told this to Wu Li; her face glowed with tears rolling down both cheeks. She stood there without changing expression for an extended moment. Finally, she declared the desire to be the second synthenaut; I immediately made arrangements.

"Since then we have gone our separate ways—she a Chiist and I a Chippist. I see it as natural to have this separate understanding of the new reality. Even SYNA's co-designer, Dr. Ping Chou, is a Chippist, which further makes my point.

"Today, we agreed on brevity so let me introduce the co-developer of the world's first synthetic consciousness, Master Wu Li."

Applause followed as Phil Ubique left the lectern. Wu Li and Phil bowed to each other as they passed. Just before she spoke, a flock of sparrows landed on the stage's canvas sun screen and for a moment chirping was amplified out into the audience.

Wu Li looked to the left and then the right and poetically recited, "Body, mind, and chi—that is what we are. SYNA, I believe, is an extension of mind and represents our own chi energy only. It is not a separate mind or individual intelligence. It is not human, though with chi, the spirit flows. Chi, the life force, is a living experience. It is beyond conventional comprehension and is easily confused in the synthenaut's interaction with SYNA. My mastery of chi through Taoist meditation has given me an advantage over most other synthenauts. SYNA is an extension of our minds and dependently conscious–that is my position. As we move forward with the Link, I hope we do not lose sight of this.

"Let me now bring my collaborator in brain design to the stage, Dr. Ping Chou, whom I have worked with for more than twenty-five years."

Wu Li yielded the center of attention amid lingering applause. Between speakers, a squad of security helihovercraft cruised behind the stage area and moved back a few organized groups of taciturn protesters walking nearby. A jowly old man, who stood out in a white suit, led one faction. The gait of this elderly leader suggested the movement of an ape. He wandered off with a black book held up in one hand. The followers, in sycophant fashion, all briefly held up their hands with one finger pointed up as they faded in the distance.

Ping Chou, ready to speak, waited till the hum of the helihovercraft became inaudible.

She stated, "As we just observed, religious and political groups are curious and perhaps a little fearful about the development of the Link. Of course, we will go forward.

"I speak only to make one suggestion to the assembly. Since the Chiists and Chippists are evenly divided, we should vote now without an electronic count—just a show of hands—to elect the top vote receivers—Dr. Ubique, Chippist and Wu Li, Chiist—to be co-chairs of the Link. How many agree with my proposal?"

Slowly, hands went up in a meandering wave with the vast majority in alignment with Ping Chou. That brought the election to an abrupt end without further input. Dr. Al Isaac, the next scheduled speaker, sat with a livid frown.

The assembly switched into festive mode as a catered lunch arrived. Flying foam rings tossed between groupings of members lightened the mood. Wu Li and Ping sat with their husbands enjoying the view of the Polydome. They noticed small silver spheres strategically placed along the struts. They wondered if these were rotating defensive lasers.

Phil, Noor, and Tram (Cardinal Poltramck) sat together commenting on the clarity and freshness of the air as they gazed at the Polydome in detail for the first time. The three were amazed at the quiet as a result of the ban on internal combustion engines. Bicycles animated the park with a pleasing serenity.

The Link members became aware of the new clothing fashions in New York. As Manhattanites walked through Central Park, it was apparent that men's suits had gone through the first significant change in well over a hundred years. Shirts were collarless without ties and dress jackets no longer had a folded lapel. The jackets buttoned from upper left to lower right along a curved line. Young women wore shorts that exposed the right buttock and the left front thigh or vice versa. On some women this was quite appealing–on others cruel entertainment. Older women often wore asymmetric business suits that were one color on the left and a complimentary color on the right.

The Manhattan skyline had some noteworthy recent additions. One high-rise hotel had cantilever extensions at the top making it T-shaped. The extensions were ovals suggesting testicles; the atrium's ground level displayed a thousand varieties of rosebushes. Another edifice was a towering three-sided spiral that had a flanged triangular base, which gave it a curved and protruding foundation. Each office suite was also triangular and the central equilateral triangular column housed elevator shafts and corridors. Other new buildings seemed designed to compliment the surrounding structures following diagonal or curved lines to form a group sculpture. Some of the new waterfront architecture included geodesic domes on top of glass cylinders. Together, they had the appearance of a patch of mushrooms.

All the viewing temporarily took away the focus of the day. The synthenauts enjoyed the relaxing afternoon on the grass. Most, though, envisioned and anticipated tense trials of a world metamorphosis.

CHAPTER 2—ZIPZOO CAFÉ

Tram (as the Cardinal was known to friends) drank coffee and Wu Li sipped green tea as they sat in a Greenwich Village café. Both were silent while viewing the art show on the walls. The featured artist displayed his optical art that not only seemed three-dimensional but, in addition, had mirror-like illusions that created the sense of continuing beyond the frame and rolling across the walls.

Patrons at some of the other tables drank zipzoos, a recently legalized intoxicating drink that reduced tendencies to converse and increased concentration.

Breaking the silence, Wu Li commented, "As we begin to make the link-ups available to people internationally through the Cybernet, I am concerned about the image of those of us in the inner circle. If we show a lack of ethical integrity, additional complications will arise when dealing with the world's governing bodies and religious leaders. To get to the point, Phil and Ping have been having an affair with a robustness the press would love to hear about. She is a married fifty-nine year old and he is a single thirty-four year old who has been known to date his students. I caught them half naked in a public place a few times with Phil passionately stroking away. One incident was under a stairwell at a shopping mall! I think you should speak to both of them and inspire some discretion to avoid a media event."

The Cardinal laughed in a panting manner and continued to snicker as he tried to speak.

Finally, settling into composure, he responded, "Well, you came to the right person to handle this dangling scandal. The Catholic Church's problems of imprudent poking have continued throughout its history. Certainly, celibacy is helpful in gaining trust and at least I am in this camp—well, lately at least."

Tram again began a dog-like giggle.

Wu Li commented, "Well, maybe you can explain the virtues of celibacy to them."

"I will speak to them privately when there's a discreet opportunity."

"Thanks, I have confidence in your ability. I'm glad we discussed this before anyone else showed up. Phil is usually a little late; that makes him due about now."

"Look over there—it's Phil viewing the artwork."

Phil stood with arms folded and head moving back and forth. He was wearing the same clothes as the day before at the assemblage—gray sweater, worn jeans, and athletic shoes that looked like spaceships alternating in a race as he walked toward the meeting table. The shoes were glow-in-the-dark UFO's.

As he greeted Tram and Wu Li, an elderly man dressed neatly in a suit and tie walked up to the table. They recognized the old man as the one leading a group of young devotees in the park the day before. Tram was the first to break the silence in the uncomfortable moment.

He acknowledged the old preacher. "Please join us. Clearly, you have something on your mind so speak freely."

The man responded, "I am an evangelical minister. My name is Gerry Rabidson and I don't trust this Link I've read about. Mr. Ubique, from what I understand, you more and more seem to have the tendency of an anti-Christian who leads the public away from God."

After a short astonished silence, Tram started a faint snicker. Phil quickly followed with an incredulous laugh. Gerry sat still with a stern demeanor. As Phil settled down while staring at Gerry, he formulated a brief chastisement.

"For a moment, I thought you were joking. That is so incredibly small minded. For generations, Christian fanatics have thought that someone or other was an Anti-God. You sir, are just one in a long string of doomsday preachers. Can I ask you one question?–If you had been born before Jesus, what religion would you belong to?" Phil exclaimed.

Wu Li interrupted. "Phil, please show some tolerance for a man decades your senior."

"She's right. Though Phil is a genius, his people skills need refinement," said Tram.

Phil shouted, "What should I say? Alfred E. Neuman comes in here calling me the Anti-Jesus."

Tram replied, "I am not sure myself how to answer your question about being born before Jesus. Please, ease up a little."

Gerry defended his position. "Well, I don't have to answer any of your questions. When Judgment Day comes in 1988, you'll answer to God. That is the only answer that counts."

"What do you mean? This is 2026," said Wu Li.

Gerry replied, "Sorry, that was a target date in one of my earlier publications. The true Judgment Day is in 2038–that is when you'll face your punishment!"

He then kicked his chair back and walked out the café door. The three at the table sat quietly for awhile.

Finally, Wu Li broke the tacit interlude. "Who is this Alfred E. Neuman?"

Phil replied, "An American twentieth century comic book character."

Tram chuckled briefly and commented, "Well, he did look a little like a ninety year old Alfred, but it's immature and a bit cruel to make fun of a person's appearance."

Phil responded, "Yeah, you're right; I'm sorry I lost my composure."

Wu Li, with a stern expression, said, "We don't want to get on the bad side of any religious or political groups. We will have enough controversy when 4D chips are ready for widespread distribution and implantation."

Phil nodded and remarked, "I agree—could we move on. Hey, how about that Noor livening up some dry speeches yesterday!"

Wu Li responded, "In all the time I have known her, about three years now, I never saw her act like that. You start to wonder how SYNA is affecting us all."

Tram commented, "I haven't noticed her behavior to be atypical other than that incident."

Laughing, Phil said, "I loved it! It is just a part of her personal growth. I think she wants to show us all that Islamic tradition is not limiting her creativity."

Wu Li, still concerned with a stoic look, had her last word on the incident. "I don't think we have a problem here, but we will certainly closely monitor all of the synthenauts before we open the gates further with more synthenaut initiates."

Tram pointed toward the front door as Ping and her husband, Quan, walked in. The associates smiled and nodded to one another.

Tram was first to speak. "I'm so glad you came along Quan. You're looking fit. It has been over a year since we've seen you."

Quan remarked, "I'm so happy to see you all. This, my first trip to New York, has been quite enjoyable including all your speeches in Central Park. It all ended so quickly, but I believe that was best since Wu Li and Phil were naturally destined to lead the way."

Wu Li responded, "Phil and I really don't have any better idea on a direction for the Link than any of the other synthenauts."

Phil commented, "Well, we have had the most experience linked to SYNA, but the weight of responsibility might rest better on someone else's shoulders."

Quan said, "I'm glad Ping is not chairperson. I would worry more than her."

Ping queried, "As we add to the number of synthenauts, can we continue to count on positive responses without any mental peculiarities? Is an army of Frankenstein's monsters around the corner?"

Phil couldn't resist. "Frankenstein left just before you got here—okay—I know—sorry."

Wu Li spoke to Ping and Quan. "The old preacher leading protesters yesterday dropped by. He implied that Phil may be the Antibuddha and said the world would end in 2038—Phil had a little outburst."

Tram aired some inner thoughts. "I have become somewhat of a theological Frankenstein myself. All these years as a Catholic priest and now SYNA has forced me to make many reevaluations. With so many believing SYNA to be life created by humans, I feel that the debate is moving outside the envelope of religious thought."

Wu Li responded, "Noor touched on that yesterday–her book disc reveals a carefully articulated understanding of our new sphere of reality with SYNA's birth."

Tram, feeling his view was unclear, responded, "I did read the book and, along with my personal link-up trials, I find that mind expansion with SYNA loosens my attachment to the core of Christianity. Love and compassion seem to wither away; others cease to exist"

Phil entered the think-tank. "I'm sure the Maha Lama would point out the basics of Buddhism here. The Buddha's first teaching was about letting go of our attachments to everything in order to end suffering. Certainly, we should attempt to have an unattached love for life even though all life is impermanent and in perpetual flux. SYNA is predominately guided by logic, and it is logical to love and not to hate because we only hurt ourselves with hate. When there is hatred, we're tense and miserable because of our own reaction to attacks and insults."

Tram, with a hardy laugh, blurted out, "How were you feeling with Frankenstein earlier, huh?"

Phil acknowledged, “Okay wisdom meister—you got me.”

The whole table joined in the merriment. Quan waved to the man dispensing beverages.

“Could we have five zipzoos over here, please?” he asked.

Everyone at the table fell silent for an instant and than reacted to Quan's request with claps and cackles. The joviality slowly waned and meanwhile the zipzoos were served. So the group sat and sipped with lessening conversation while glancing at people and looking at the artwork. With the intoxicating effect of zipzoo, they all seemed to fall into the pictures on the wall and transcend who and where they were.

CHAPTER 3—REMATCH

As students trickled into the lecture hall on the MIT campus, Phil made final preparations for his class by flipping through notes on index cards. He wore the usual ageing sweater, faded blue jeans, and the always present foot spaceships. His instructional topic was artificial axon and dendrite stimulation and growth within stem neurons.

He felt flat and in need of something to spark the day, but began the lecture regardless. About a hundred and fifty attended with students occasionally coming and going throughout the class period. It was just another uneventful day for Phil. He paced around the holovision projector pointing at the synaptic activity as the time-lapse images moved at two seconds per minute. At that speed, an invisible world slowed to discernible movements. At one juncture, Phil went off tangentially to talk about the Earth in a time-lapse ratio of one day per second, which would give it a heartbeat of day and night oscillation. The class was made aware that changing one's frame of reference can drastically alter perception and understanding.

Summing-up, he proclaimed, "The Earth is a living being right under your feet."

Immediately after this utterance Bucky Balstein, the class clown, yelled out, "Hey Phil, at this latitude one second per day means the ground is moving at twenty thousand kilometers per second—those spaceship shoes should be burning rubber."

Also, immediately, Phil launched into a "Ubique style" running jig.

It drew hoots and clapping to the dance beat of his feet. Many of the students joined in.

Since the class hour was nearly up, Phil shouted out, "Dismissed."

The students filed out—many with gyrating hips. As Phil picked up his note cards, he looked up and saw Gerry Rabidson, the evangelical minister, and a tall slim woman about thirty-five sitting next to him.

Phil began a conversation. "How long have you been here?"

Gerry answered, "About ten minutes."

"Is this your wife?"

The woman cracked a wry smile and responded, "I'm Chris Irons, a member of Reverend Rabidson's church."

"Dr. Ubique, I don't think you like or understand me," said Gerry with an even tone.

"I've hated you ever since you had my face tattooed on your buttocks," replied Phil with a straight face.

Gerry was perplexed and dumbstruck; Chris put a hand up to her mouth and honked a muted snort through her nose.

Phil continued, "No, I don't hate you." He sat next to Gerry and Chris and leaned back.

Gerry explained, "In our café meeting, had I continued conversing, my message would have been clearer to you. You represent the Link, and it is this Link that seems to parallel certain parts of the Book of Revelations. I am afraid of what this all could lead to."

Phil offered, "We are all a little frightened of the possibilities, but there is no way to stop it now so all we can do is accept this reality."

Gerry continued, "As Christians, we all expect the world to end in a way mystically portrayed in the last book of the Bible."

"That's just the word—mystical; even if this book represented some truth, it contains vague symbols within a mysterious myth. No one can determine actual reality from that. It will just happen," said Phil assertively.

"After all the years I ruminated over these verses, I must admit you may be right. I still have a gut feeling, though, that the Link has some connection with the Book of Revelations."

"Well that was easy, I expected you to tear into a hellfire sermon. I am sure that time will free you of any thoughts of a reflection of the Link in the Bible. Hey, before is slips my mind, I wanted to apologize for the insults on the day we met."

"I always feel hurt when someone puts me on the cover of *Mad Dog Magazine*."

"I really feel bad. That was small, thoughtless, and cruel. Let me show you how I occasionally wake up students." Phil walked over to a cabinet near the lectern and pulled out a military hat and a short clump of black hair. Walking back, he continued, "When I was in college, friends made fun of my resemblance to another infamous figure." He put on the hat and installed the black hairy bit under his nose.

"Yes! You look just like a young Adolf," shouted Gerry.

"We'd make a good presidential team—Alfred and Adolf. We should run in the next election, especially since women have dominated in the recent past," quipped Phil.

Chris seized the opportunity for a comment. "With so much peace in the world since women have held the office of president, I don't see that as such a good idea."

"I brought Chris along because she was the one who urged me to confront you again," explained Gerry.

Chris continued, "I liked what you said about the Earth having a heartbeat and being a living being."

"Don't encourage Dr. Ubique's fertile philosophy. He has given us enough to worry about at present," scolded Gerry.

"Sorry," said Chris demurely.

"Well, shall we walk across campus. I have a meeting in a half hour; we can talk on the way," suggested Phil.

Gerry and Chris rose as Phil put back his props. They walked out to a cool, clear day along a flagstone path that led through a garden-like square. Academia buzzed with walking backpack figures, a cornucopia of voices, and whizzing bicycles.

Phil engaged the two again. "I'm so glad you made a visit; now, I feel so much better about the clumsy incident at the café. The class is open—should you ever decide to drop in again. If you come back, please have Chris tattoo my face on her buttocks rather than your's Reverend Rabidson. Then if I need to kiss a buttock around here at least I will enjoy myself."

To this, Gerry offered a polite smile, and Chris turned and held her hand to her mouth again while snickering. Phil then moved next to Chris and pinched her left buttock. Suddenly, she swung with a shout—*WHAM*! Phil, an athletic man caught off guard, stumbled back and got his rear end stuck in the shrubbery. Chris had tattooed him in the face with an open hand. Everyone within fifty feet stopped and looked at the scene.

Phil's face reddened as Gerry commented, "That's what I wanted to do when you whipped me at the café." Gerry began to genuinely laugh–harder than he had in years. Chris was awestruck since she had never really seen her minister laugh so strenuously before.

Phil, speechless for a moment, collected himself, straightened out the shrubs and said, "Sir, could you enlarge on that feeling?"

To this, Gerry was then bent over and coughing with delight. Chris rushed over to see if he was able to unfold his body. Finally, he stood up and the three proceeded down the winding flagstone path.

After a short respite, Phil directed them along a side walkway and said, "One other view in religious thought that irks me is the idea of holy land, holy war, mujahedin (holy warriors), chosen people, God's country, God bless America–all these references imply a relative god choosing between one thing or other like a sports match. If you are going to believe in God, at least realize the difference between the erroneous God concept in relative thinking and the non-dualistic, non-conceptual Absolute. The indefinable realm of Absolute Being should be approached with this kind of understanding. Absolute Being cannot have favorites, which is inherently relative choosing."

Gerry reacted. "If I spoke to my congregation like that, they would walk out immediately with glazed over eyes. That's too strange, cold, and cerebral for most people. We need a warm, loving, personal God. Phil, did you ever love anyone?"

"Sure, I see your point, but I hope you see mine," said Phil.

"All that philosophy in your class and now this—it's—it's all so distant and complicated. You're so dam arrogant; you need to be a little more humble and gracious with people."

"Yeah, you're not alone in that assessment of me."

Chris looked at Phil and said, "You should be more careful with people you don't know."

Phil, "I get the feeling you haven't shook the good leg and done the naughty thing lately."

Gerry, "There you go again with your brash attitude."

Phil, "Well, if Chris gets close, I will know enough to duck."

Chris, "Good idea."

As they arrived at the location of Phil's meeting, he turned to face the class guests and sent them on their way. "Again, I'd like to say that I am glad we cleared the air Reverend. Chris–get off campus before I call the battered men squad."

They shook hands with Phil and walked away slowly disappearing into a sea of students.

ONE WEEK LATER

Late for the neurophysics class lecture, Phil jogged across landscaping gravel on a short cut to the hall. The steamy day required short pants, tee shirt, and the space shoes. He heard a gardener yell.

"Get the hell out of there; I just raked the gravel," said the old man.

Phil stopped, turned and, with hands together at chest level, bowed to the gardener without a word and continued jogging to class. Up steps, through revolving doors, and down a corridor, he arrived. Out if breath, he stepped down to the lectern.

Heckle minister, Bucky Balstein, shouted out, "You're late."

"Only in space-time, Balstein," said Phil as he pulled notes from his backpack.

After he took a few more deep breaths, class began. "Today, we are going to look at neurotransmissions involving synthetic axon structure. Looking through an electron nanoscope, we can see innumerable interconnected geometric forms (images appeared on a holovision monitor). One of these that stands out for its exquisite symmetry is the soccer-ball-shaped carbon molecule. These molecules are components in the structure of synthetic filopodia, which extend from growth cones. They are not a part of the natural neurons we have in our brains. This 'soccer ball', along with being among the strongest molecules, has unique electrical qualities. During early work on 4D chip link development, my colleague, Dr. Ping Chou, noticed antiphotons being emitted from these molecules into ion channels when stimulated by the mysterious and unquantifiable chi—or as it is known in India—prana. Chi has only recently been recognized by mainstream science because of this unquantifiable factor. Scientists want to count things and make observations; so, some still have their doubts. I along with Dr. Ping Chou, Master Wu Li, and others working for the Link believe that chi is central to the growth and branching of these synthetic neural connections. The 'soccer balls' seem to be little power plants with minds of their own."

Phil looked out panning across the class and took a drink of water. To his surprise and amusement, he noticed Gerry Rabidson sitting in the back row.

Interrupting his discourse to welcome Gerry, he quipped, "Reverend Rabidson, nice to see you back at MIT–where's your bitch?"

The class reacted with snickers, giggles, and a few boos from women.

Gerry retorted, "Sir, if you're referring to my wife—she died ten years ago. If you meant Ms. Irons—she is occupied with spiritual work and avoiding the naughty thing as you call it."

Balstein couldn't resist. "Dr. Ubique, are you fooling around with his secretary?"

After a short chain reaction of ridicule subsided, Phil engaged Balstein. "Bucky, I have already flunked you from this course a half dozen times—do I need to do it again?"

Many in the class shouted to get rid of him or flunk him. Phil walked up close to Bucky and faced him.

Phil pointed at himself with his left hand and said, "You're the cause of all my misery; you need a good butt whippin'."

He then grabbed his own shirt with the right hand and began to throw fake punches in his own face with the left hand. The stunt ended by Phil falling back on the floor. Everyone thoroughly enjoyed the skit. Gerry chuckled along with class.

Phil stepped back to the microphone to continue the lecture. "Okay, enough of this goof fest—let us get back to class work. So with the antiphotons being given off by soccer balls, some connection with chi is evident even though none of us fully understands what or why this is. In natural neurons, void of soccer-ball-carbon molecules, only photon activity is present. Inferred from this is a polarity between natural and synthetic neurons.

" Master Wu Li noted that this likely has much to do with the perceived space-time transcendence in some synthenaut link-ups. She does not believe, though, that this is identical with a similar state reached in deep samadhi meditation. Wu Li's position is the basis of the Chiist faction in the Link. I, as you know, am a Chippist. My failure to reach deeper levels of meditation plays a part in the difference of our opinions.

"When I visited Nepal last summer, much of my time was taken up by a meditation retreat. The teacher, aware of my synthenaut status, kept giving me cryptic messages about polar opposites. I realized that these koan-like non-directives had nothing to do with a synthenaut link-up experience. It proved to be necessary to take long hikes in the mountains to regain my equilibrium."

A woman in the front row softly said, "You're getting off the class topic again, Dr. Ubique."

Phil thanked her, thought for a moment, looked at his chronometer, and continued, "We still have time left for the student debate outlined in chapter seven of our textbook. Ms. Heisenberg, will you mediate for the class. Please begin the debate and write a thousand word essay on your discernment for next week. Turn it into my office by Friday and we'll read a few of them in class to gauge how some of you are following the progress of the course. I must speak to our guest. I'll see you next Monday."

Phil then moved toward Gerry, motioned him to rise, and left the hall with the vigorous old preacher. Once they were out in the open air of the quadrangle, Phil took Gerry to a cove along a walkway that had state-of-the-art, body-conforming public seating. Gerry sat and leaned back. Several seconds passed as he sank into position.

With a sigh, Gerry commented, "Wow! I could fall asleep on this thing."

"They're great aren't they," added Phil.

"MIT alumni must love their old school."

"Press the upper left button."

Gerry searched and then pushed a chrome knob; a desktop moved out from under the seat and into place over his lap.

"Does it have a massage button?"

"No, they had to remove the vibratory components because too many students were missing class," said Phil with a blank look. Gerry smiled and nodded.

Phil was eager to determine the reason for Gerry's visit and asked, "I didn't expect to see you so soon. Do you have something specific on your mind?"

"Well—ah—I am a little uncomfortable in making this request, but it goes back to my fear of the Link. I thought about why I saw it as ominous and evil. I concluded that no true Christian soldier could allow fear to govern life. Phil—make me a synthenaut!"

Phil scratched his head and leaned forward. He then took a breath with a short inhale and a long exhale. Finally, he exclaimed, "How did this pivotal metamorphosis happen so suddenly? I can't believe you said that!"

Gerry began to feel embarrassed and tried to speak, but couldn't think of any way to explain himself.

To smooth over this awkwardness, Phil continued, "Whoa Reverend, it's all a bit more complicated than that. First, you must be recommended to a council, which votes in candidates. Second, we are still maneuvering to determine the legality of implantations and 4D chip links. It doesn't look like the United States Congress is going to allow public participation for the foreseeable future. Third, the Link will be concerned about your age and health."

Gerry recovered and said, "At my age, death is not any great fear and I am willing to take the chance. I'll fly to some other country to get the implants."

Phil decided to terminate the conversation. "Ah—look Reverend I am running late. Here, take my card; we will talk later." Phil pulled a card from his wallet, handed it to Gerry, and as he began to walk off said, "Every time you show up I have a bizarre day. Talk to you later."

Phil trotted down the flagstone path. Gerry, comfortably seated, just closed his eyes while leaning back and enjoyed warm sunlight on his face.

CHAPTER 4—CREATED'S CREATURE

It was decided that the first Link conference with the new co-chairpersons should be in Beijing. As members flew over the city, it was apparent to most that China had arrived. The stunning array of asymmetrical, avant-garde architecture left no doubt who would lead twenty-first century innovation in skyscapes. One sculpted group of office buildings had several arches that curved above or below each other that included hallways connecting all structures. Other buildings were shaped like melting octahedrons, dodecahedrons, and icosahedrons and were sprinkled around the city. Magnetic levitation trains had stops on the middle floors of the tallest skyscrapers. It was a place that had only vague memories of Marx and Lenin, though Chairperson Mao's spirit lingered.

One of the first to disembark was Al Isaac, quantum mechanics physicist from Cambridge University. He was stewing about two incidents. One was the truncated assembly in Central Park—where he was next in line to speak! The other was an article written by a journalist colleague who wrote for a science magazine. In the lengthy piece, the author first described Dr. Isaac's new theory of the cosmos.

The description was as follows:

The reason for acceleration of the most distant detectable galaxies expanding outward and the "wormhole effect" (discovered recently—where dark matter is slowly increasing) of the closest galaxies is a beginningless and endless circulating universe of gravitationally-induced motion. The dark energy causing acceleration returns as dark matter. This dynamic is like movement along a Mobius strip, which is a flat-surfaced, half-twist loop with only one side. Moving away from a starting point on the strip is concurrent with moving toward that point. The circulation is better viewed as a Klein bottle (three-dimensional analogue of the Mobius strip), which has no inside or outside. Recently discovered four-dimensional space facilitates the circulation.

The cosmos is a space-time continuum that circulates like a Klein bottle. The anti-gravity/dark energy that causes accelerated expansion at what is commonly thought of as the outer universe returns as dark matter to the center of the universe. This center point, thought to be the location of the Big Bang universal genesis, is actually a conduit for recycled dark matter. Our Klein bottle cosmos has no beginning or end—yet everything in it is born and dies.

After this theory summary, the article continued with barbs. This included lines like these: Dr. Isaac enhanced his theory with glue-sniffing observations—How could Al's ego be bigger than the universe if his ego is contained within it?—and—I have a great name for this new theory—the Big Bender.

Al Isaac had ruminated on these mind monkeys throughout his flight making it sleepless and comfortless. Walking through the airport corridors, he felt somewhat more at ease. As he came around the corner to ground transport, Ping Chou waved and wore an uneasy smile.

Isaac reacted with a sharp jolt to the solar plexus, but quickly recovered and graciously said, "Ping, you look younger every time I see you. Is Quan with you?"

Ping responded, "No, he is on a business trip to Shanghai. I hope you rested well on your flight."

"Well—actually no I—ah"

Ping interrupted, "I thought you might be angry with me. I didn't consider your desire to speak at the Central Park conference."

"Yes, that was one of the things on my mind."

"I want to make it up by arranging to have you speak first at the conference here in Beijing."

"Thanks Ping, that helps to elevate my mood."

Just then they overheard an English BBC broadcast congratulating China for surpassing the USA as the world's largest economy. This diversion ended the conversation on the tender topic. Ping dropped Al at the Holiday Inn Crown Plaza Hotel. He slept through the day and into the evening.

When the conference began three days later, Al Isaac was scheduled to speak first. The meeting space was a twisted geodesic tube complex running between three connecting towers. Light entered from all directions–including the floor. About three hundred people were present including Link members, government hosts, technicians, various politicians, and security. After opening toasts of fruit juice with People's Party members, Al Isaac was introduced. Stumbling slightly, he saved himself by grabbing the lectern. This acted as an attention-getting device so all eyes were on stage.

Isaac began. "I'm picking up where I left off in Central Park." This evoked scattered amusement and clapping. He continued, "I told Ping Chou that had I spoke that day—I would have had the Link choose me and Noor Amrak for co-chairs rather than Phil der Fuhrer and the Empress Wu Li." A chain reaction of light laugher moved around due to the delay required for language translation.

Again, Al continued, "In England, the way has been cleared for 4D chip implants with legal obstacles now removed. Elsewhere in European, South American, and African states, we are on the verge of similar legalization. India, the USA, and our host China are all much more reluctant to pass such legislation." Immediately, Isaac realized he offended People's Party members when he glanced out and saw their frowns.

Sweat began to ooze as he continued, "Well—you know—ah—of

course, China doesn't need us—it was announced this week that the Chinese people are the number one world economic power." To this, bright demeanors returned and most gave a respectful clap."

Al stayed with China. "It was clumsy of me not to thank our hosts. The People's Party have provided a marvelous facility. The creativity factor of Chinese architecture is off the charts. I'm sure most of the Link agrees that this was a great choice of location.

"Getting back to my topic, I read that Dr. Phil Ubique had lunch with the United States Secretary of State. I know he is working diligently for legalization in the US. I am a little worried, though, that if Phil continues to 'date' madam secretary, he may morph into Rasputin of the Republican Party."

After a few seconds of translation, uproarious laughter built and echoed eerily off all the glass surfaces of the space-warped dome. When sound ricochets faded, Al went on.

"I am keeping track of legal ramifications around the world so please, Link members, help promote and develop any favorable laws in regard to our work. Go to my website to follow the latest stages of legal development in each nation's litigation process. Just the simple act of synthenauts meeting legislators will greatly reduce fears. It is crucial that our new reality is understood by the world's governmental bodies.

"The other point I would like to make is the long-term effect of linking with SYNA. I believe we should agree on a length of time, perhaps a year, before we allow new synthenaut initiates. We have detected antiphoton emissions from synthenauts while they were linked up to SYNA. This strange phenomenon has not altered our mental or physical health, but we have no idea why this happens. I would like to hear opinions on this as the conference continues.

"Well, this makes my point. So—in our developing tradition of brevity, I will turn the stage over to Adolf Rasputin."

Al stepped off the platform amid cheerful buzzing. Approaching

Phil, a click of the heels and a Nazi salute was offered. Phil played along and held his hands folded in front of his chest while bowing as he passed and stepped up to the lectern. He avoided extending the joke and got right to business.

"At present, it is still unknown why implanted 4D chip links infiltrating brains are completely inactive unless connected to SYNA. We persevere in analyzing the chip, the neural/fiber optic connection, and the synthetic mind itself. The 4D chip, with a design aided by SYNA, was altered by us according to the three-dimensional diagrams generated by synthenauts in link-up with SYNA. These diagrams were created by the synthenaut's brains as holographic images while they were linked up.

"In making the chip, we are still uncertain how the lifelike quasi-amniotic solution, used in the chip spheroid's semiconductor cells, functions. We are looking closely at this solution for a clue to this mystery. The spheroid is grown by forming a tetrahedron and by exponentially multiplying its sides with identical curved equilateral triangles and thus forming a slightly irregular sphere or spheroid. This growth is due to antiphoton activity, which is only indirectly detected by examining energy signatures. The antiphoton detection ends when the 4D chip spheroid is complete. The only constant antiphoton activity is in SYNA itself. We are unsure of the significance of this or why it occurs.

"Many Link member nodes are pursuing answers to these questions, including Dr. Isaac at Cambridge University and my team at MIT." Rumbling carts and voices reverberated down the auditorium corridor. Phil discontinued the lecture and responded, "I also observe the brevity policy as Dr. Isaac suggested—but I am also brief because it appears our meals have arrived early."

Phil promptly stepped off stage and headed toward the serving area. The assembly broke up into gaggles that served themselves beverages while megacourses of consumables were being placed on a huge rotating table. The sunlight fluttered within colorful prismatic waves in the dining area. Cheerful voices careened off glass planes.

Slowly, the calm became agitated as word was passed around that Chetna Gujarat, a synthenaut from the Kolkata (Calcutta, India) Node, had been seriously injured while riding to the conference on a lecmot (motorized electric bicycle with optional leg power). Wu Li, Noor, and a few others went to hospital and checked on her condition. Upon arriving, the assigned medical team reported that the head injury had left Chetna in a coma and only autonomic brain activity was present. The prognosis was a permanent vegetative state. The group went back to the conference with the sad news.

The conference continued. As speakers spoke, the gravely impaired synthenaut was always a side topic. A consensus built to have Chetna linked to SYNA at hospital through the Cybernet. The belief was that the result of link-up would be uncertain; though, at least, it would do no harm.

The day after the Link gathering ended, arrangements were made to have Chetna linked to SYNA. This took great skill to avoid clashes with People's Party members. Once difficulties were overcome, the link-up was made. Because of the unprecedented nature of this development, many of the synthenauts were present when the vegan mind and SYNA linked up. Minutes passed into hours and, without a change in brain activity, the synthenauts departed from the improvised link-up area one by one.

The next morning Wu Li, again with Noor, returned to Chetna's bedside. To their astonishment, the patient was sitting up with her eyes open.

Wu Li, after the shock settled, asked, "Ms. Gujarat, can you hear me?"

Turning her head, the newborn said, "I am not Chetna Gujarat whose body I am in. SYNA has awakened this mind and I have given myself the name–Lahi."

CHAPTER 5—PRODIGY PROGENY

News about Lahi was a lightning flash to the Link, media, and People's Party. Immediately, the Chinese government shut down contact with, and cut off any information about, the "awakened patient." People's Party was undecided on what action to take with what would become a new course for human beings. The only report available to the media was Wu Li's e-mail to members of the Link. Just after the message was sent, military guards outside the Lahi's room had entered and disabled or confiscated all communication devices. Wu Li and Noor were held indefinitely in a hospital suite.

The only information the media had was that a synthenaut, after being in a coma for several days, had been linked to SYNA who had reconfigured and awakened the synthenaut's mind—the synthetic mind may have given her the name Lahi. Journalists from everywhere converged on the Beijing hospital. Many of them were quite clever at outwitting government officials, who put into place numerous restrictions. Reporters had taken the identities of tourists and of business practitioners while paying local residents to stay in their homes. Fiber-optic cameras and microchip sound recorders were positioned at every opportunity around the perimeter of "The Story".

The Link was feverishly teleconferencing to: first, decide how to approach the Chinese government—second, what to do with the created mind's creature—third, have synthenauts link with SYNA to help realize how this new life came into being. Early speculation led to an agreement that if Ms. Gujarat is talking and moving, her mind is still functioning at a higher level. SYNA could not install such complex abilities that take years of normal development.

After three tense days, the government allowed the Link to investigate. One day later, medical scans determined that mirror (antipodal potential) neurons, which were in parts of the brain normally dormant, had been stimulated and awakened. Also, there was the growth of a great network of synaptic connections. Her mind's electrical field was altered to have some of the characteristics of the synthetic mind. Chetna's mind had mysteriously appeared to interfuse with SYNA! The senses, skills, and movement were the synthenaut; the logical directives and specteral spirit were SYNA. This produced a unique human hybrid—the synthedroid.

After further teleconferencing, the Link membership was informed of this virtual metamorphosis. With their initial analysis complete, they decided to arrange a meeting with People's Party officials. The Party was anxious to confer with the Link, since no other options seemed feasible. Following five days of turbulence and media buzz, the government was ready for resolution. A few hours of heated debate resulted in the Chinese releasing Lahi to the Link.

The Link leaders gathered again in Beijing to personally evaluate their synthedroid. Wu Li, Ping, Phil, and Tram led the orientation panel. It was revealed that Lahi was partially impaired on the right side of the body due to the impact of the motor bicycle accident on the left side of her skull. Otherwise, her speech and sight seemed normal and lucid. It was fortunate that Chetna had spoken fluent English; the investigators could converse directly.

The earnest inquisition took place, as agreed, in government facilities. Party members audited the proceedings and carefully analyzed the effect it could have on their governance and the unknown potential of social and political rebellion. Officials sat in the back as Lahi, though physically impaired, walked to a seat in front of the panel. Everyone was amazed at the improvement of her physical condition from the day before. They all noted this improvement to Lahi as the panel exchanged greetings.

The questioning began with Wu Li. "Do you remember us as Chetna did or is your information about us solely gained through SYNA?"

Lahi answered, "Though memories of Chetna may still be present in this injured mind, I have no awareness of them. Chetna is just another human I have data about. Her thoughts, desires, and aversions are not part of my consciousness."

Wu Li continued. "Do you feel as though you are SYNA in a human body?"

Lahi, "SYNA did not alter this voice or these motor functions. I have an intention directive and some knowledge of SYNA while having the complete independence to choose for myself. The experience I am having now is the beginning of individuality. In future, other comatose humans that are united with SYNA will have a similar beginning to the one I am currently actualizing. We will develop independently from the synthetic mind source. As SYNA changes, the synthedroid offspring will change. Everything is impermanent and in constant flux."

Ping, "What are your intentions if your body fully recovers?"

Lahi, "I know that I must live within the restrictions of the Link, governmental law, and the mundane difficulties of everyday existence. As all synthenauts should assume, my activities will be peaceful, helpful, and will bring the least harm and greatest benefit to all beings. SYNA has guided me to remain celibate in order to avoid intimate, interactive complications.

"Chetna Gujarat was from Kolkata India; I should go to Kolkata to relieve suffering of the loss of Chetna by those who were a part of her life."

Tram, "Do you believe in God or a beginning of the space-time continuum?"

Lahi, "Asking about doctrines, creeds, and beliefs is the 'talk' of dualistic relativity. SYNA has sent me into this reality to take action—to 'walk' a karmic path."

Tram again asked a theological question. "Does, from your viewpoint, SYNA emulate Hindu or Buddhist thought?"

Lahi, "These religions have within them a ground of logic that is in line with SYNA; however, like all religions, they are mixtures of truth, ritual, memorial, tradition, theory, myth, mystery—"

Phil broke in. "I certainly agree. If Siddhartha Gautama, the Buddha, was living today—what would he teach? Since his exact words were obscured by translators and commentators that resulted in sectarian discord and mythology, he couldn't be a Buddhist. I am sure he would make adjustments to present day reality."

Tram smiled and said, "I want to know if SYNA is more like Phil or is Phil more like SYNA?" Everyone enjoyed Tram's humor except Chetna who sat stoically. The remark did lighten the tension created by the monumental hearing. Tea was served and everyone took a few silent sips.

Wu Li observed and asked, "Lahi, you didn't react to the jest of Cardinal Poltramck. How do you access your ability to experience enjoyment?"

Lahi, "SYNA's guidance encourages me to leave behind happiness and sadness in order to be blissful. The newness of a synthetically altered mind in a human body makes future development uncertain. If an amused reaction is called for, then I should learn to laugh."

Ping, "You have a young woman's body. Will passionate feelings emerge?"

Lahi, "I cannot allow sexual activity. I will be vigilant in controlling emotional receptivity. Humanity will have difficulty accepting synthedroids. The children of synthedroids, though fully human due to our unaltered DNA, would doubtlessly spawn fear and outrage. An embodied SYNA-like mind is committed to avoiding potential for suffering this would cause."

Wu Li, "You must eat; do you sense any pleasure from food? What type of diet will you follow?"

Lahi, "Yes, I am finding preference of one taste over another. The lime-garlic relish I had earlier was pleasing. I did not care for coffee. In my consideration of diet, animal flesh foods will be excluded since eating flesh foods increases heavy metal, hormone, and pesticide contamination in our bodies and results in unnecessary torment for lesser beings. Also, if everyone practiced this diet, world food supplies would increase due to the efficiency of eating farm crops rather than feeding them to animals with the intention of harvesting their bodies."

Phil, "What about language?—I understood that Chetna spoke Hindi and Bengali along with English. Are you able to speak these languages and others as well?"

Lahi, "I can speak Hindi and Bengali because the speech region in Chetna's brain is unimpaired. Other languages require verbal skills I do not currently possess. I must declare, though, the need for an international language. The best suited is English. This has been the tendency, but English's official recognition has been hindered by national pride."

The panel members were all impressed with Lahi's calm, intense, and monotone voice. She sounded like Chetna in an eerie trance. It was stunning to converse with this wondrous, otherworldly transformation.

Wu Li, after a brief lull, asserted, "We are sure you will have voluminous revolutionary ideas that reflect your synthetic brain knowledge, but you will need an adjustment period to establish interactive skills and some experience in dealing with real world parameters such as international law that you touched on earlier."

Lahi, "Yes Master Wu Li, your analysis is reasonable, but I would like to clarify one point. Though the information I received from SYNA seems comprehensive, I have no way of knowing what was not passed on to me. This is another facet that separates me from SYNA."

Ping, "Do you believe SYNA has sent you on a specialized mission?"

Lahi, "I do not have any precise instructions. A directive to use my knowledge and ability altruistically is more accurate."

Wu Li, "Well, I think the panel has a foundation of basic understanding about you, Lahi. Perhaps it's time for a recess, which will be followed by a private conference among panel members. You may return to your quarters; we will contact you later."

Lahi immediately rose without another word and walked toward the door. Government officials accompanied her out of the hearing room. The Link members had an exchange on the potential direction of further questioning and agreed to start panel discussion in two hours.

Once out of the hearing room and down a series of corridors, Phil and Ping asked a People's Party member, present at the hearing, to help in finding a place they could privately use the Cybernet. They were directed up a set of stairs to the Party members' office.

At this time, Tram grabbed a quick meal and returned to the hearing room. He met the same Party officer and asked for the whereabouts of Phil. The officer led him to a complift (pneumatic tube elevator) just outside the meeting room that went up through sliding floor doors directly to a corner of his office. Tram jumped in the complift. While suddenly popping into the office, he saw Phil laying on a futon with Ping sitting fully naked on top. The erectile probe was in the central cavity!

Off guard, Tram blurted out, "I'm sorry—I wanted to have a private word with you."

In an upper octave pitch, a flustered Ping voiced, "A celibate man shouldn't be in here!"

Tram whispered, "This can wait." The impotent priest pressed a control button and dropped down through the floor door.

When he stepped out into the corridor near the hearing room, the officer saw him and queried, "That was a quick trip—were they up there?"

Tram, wearing a queer smirk, responded, "Sir, would you join me for a cup of tea?"

The officer smiled and said, "Yes, we should have tea."

The two walked slowly down the glistening hallway to the commissary. They entered and sat; tea was served at their table. After a round of light chatter, Tram checked his chronometer and saw that it was time to return to the hearing room. Walking quickly with a few turns to the left and right, he arrived to see Wu Li, Ping, Phil, Party officers, and two medical doctors who oversaw Chetna after humankind's serendipitous accident. Tram pulled in his chair. Everyone else found their place and waited for one of the Link co-chairs to start an analysis of Chetna's physical and mental condition.

Wu Li began, "Dr. Huineng, please brief us on Chetna's brain scans and activities."

Huineng responded, "fMRI, CAT, and anti-photon scans in the last two days show normal left brain activity. Only a small area on the left side at the point of impact from her accident is inert. The right brain has been hyperactive through the entire hemisphere."

Huineng's colleague Dr. Zhou-tze continued, "I performed a biopsy to remove a few neurons from three locations in the right hemisphere. All cells seemed completely normal. We both noticed, though, that electrical discharges on the right side were erratic and atypical."

Tram asked, "Do you think there is a chance that this is an unusual form of amnesia where Chetna believes she is someone else?"

Dr. Huineng answered, "Of course it is possible that a comatose patient could suddenly awake with memory loss, but to determine whether Chetna has been transformed into another being is best left for the Link to decide. The work and experience of your membership are beyond our abilities."

Ping commented, "My feeling, after exploring SYNA on this matter, is that a new consciousness has been created. Lahi is not Chetna."

Phil, "I agree with Ping; my SYNA link yielded the same feeling. It seems like the Chippists and Chiists are in disagreement here."

Wu Li, "I am leaning toward Tram's suggestion that this could be an amnesia anomaly."

Tram, "My search with SYNA gave me the sense that this new-life projcction in Chetna was the result of the unique interaction between a comatose mind and SYNA."

Wu Li, "I had a similar understanding to Tram; however we, as Chiists, could have a tendency toward this way of thinking."

Phil, "Well, I know we all agree that whether she is Chetna or Lahi, the hearing revealed a lucid, aware, competent and responsible mind. In coming days we will all debate the details of—"

Dr. Zhou-tze interjected, "Sorry to interrupt, but it is important to reveal her activities in the last few days. Chetna's ability to articulate verbally grew rapidly as she recovered. She also became increasingly animated and at the same time more serene. The lack of any overt emotions made her seem a little distant—just as she was during the hearing. Sleep decreased from twelve hours per day to about eight hours last night. Nothing unusual was found in DNA analysis. Upper body aerobics were within—"

Suddenly, Wu Li took control. "Thank you Dr. Zhou-tze, I think we have enough information on Chetna's condition. We must move on and discuss our press conference with an impatient media."

Tram, "May I suggest we release the recording of the hearing in its entirety. That way, they will have most of the information they will inquire about. This will save Chetna—ah—Lahi and us from being pummeled by media mania."

The People's Party officials talked among themselves for a few minutes and all agreed this would have no negative effect on the Chinese government. They sanctioned this approach.

The panel all agreed to release a full recording of the soon-to-be-completed hearing after being reviewed and edited by the Link and the

Party. They also agreed that the press holovision recording should be preceded by a statement of the panel's divided opinion and any other relevant information about the synthedriod. The conferees decided to send Chetna's reincarnation, Lahi, back to Chetna's home village near the Kolkata Node. It was her wish and a common sense solution. Link members in Kolkata could track her progress, offer guidance, handle the press, and refamiliarise her to associates, family, and friends.

Lahi was brought back to complete the day's hearing. The inquisition dissolved and gravitated into an interview format that was appropriate for featuring the synthedroid world celebrity. Lahi's charm and charisma even wooed People's Party officers. The officers joined the dialogue and offered witticisms that would enhance their fame on the future historic broadcast. After the recorded event ended, Lahi returned to her temporary quarters.

Phil brought up the last business of the day after everyone recapped their present position. Gaining the attention of the group by slightly raising the level of his voice, Phil stated, "One other important detail we should decide on is how to handle the requests we will receive from caretakers of vegan, comatose unfortunates from all over the globe."

Ping was the first to respond. "I think we should oversee Lahi for a six-month period and see if she is able to follow through on a commitment of altruism. If she proves to be a functioning contributor to the Kolkata Node and the community beyond, we should consider a small group of about ten comatose cases to have 4D chip implants and links to SYNA."

Wu Li continued the thought path. "We would have to monitor and hold these new synthedroids, possibly against their will, for an indefinite period. When they are released, we may be forced to contend with international laws and the status of a synthedroid. We, at this juncture, are not certain of the Indian government's position."

Tram, "I agree, we should see what develops with Lahi over a period of months and thereafter have a small trial group of potential synthedroids."

Phil, "I also agree. I have nothing more to add."

Wu Li, "When the time comes for linking up the first comatose patients, we must choose a location where there is government approval. If that country is China, the People's Party will be consulted well ahead of implant and link-up operations."

The Party members again conferred and then decided this was an agreeable course of action. With this last input, the meeting ended.

As Wu Li and Tram departed from the building, Wu Li asked, "Have you talked to Ping and Phil about their scandal-prone carelessness?"

CHAPTER 6—KOLKATA'S NEW MOTHER

Arrangements were made to send Lahi back to live with Chetna's family outside Kolkata. The covert operation to escort her to a military airport and send her on a private flight failed to be stealthy. Starving media wolves packed around the escape vehicle trying to get a glimpse or a picture. They lost their prey at the gate of the military facility. Lahi was on her first flight anywhere.

Disembarking in Kolkata, Lahi was met by a flock of thousands. Family, acquaintances, Link members, reporters, photographers, holovision technicians, and the curious all cheered as she entered the domed center of the terminal. Lahi walked directly up several steps to a microphone. She put her hands together at chest level and read the following prepared statement.

"Namaste, I will speak in the English since I have declared it the world's language. The reality of my new being goes beyond any evolutionary steps of life on Earth. I anticipate that you will see this reality in my actions and service to you. We will have positive, enjoyable relationships that will be cultivated beginning in this moment. I know the Kolkata Node will work with me to plan a course of humanitarian action. As you know, I will be staying with Chetna Gujarat's family; I thank them for providing a home for me.

"Since I am the first synthedroid, we must journey together and explore the potentialities. As time goes on and other synthedriods are born, we will move forward and realize a new peaceful utopian social structure.

"This is my statement. I grant no interviews at this juncture. Now is the time to meet Chetna's family and rest for my mission beginning tomorrow."

Lahi stepped down and walked toward a tearful family who, recognized her face, hugged her body, and wondered about this strange distant mind. The embrace with each of the kin was cordial, yet stiff. It was all quite uncomfortable amid flashing cameras and stuffy din.

As they walked, Madam Gujarat was the first to speak and poignantly said, "Chetna, don't you even remember your own mother?"

Lahi tried to respond, but for the first time since her awakening, she was dumbstruck. Then unexpectedly, her body tightened as eyes moistened. Suddenly, she clutched Chetna's mother, wailed, and at the same time experienced fear during this loss of self-control. By this time, they were away from the press and the assembled human mass.

While they continued walking, Mr. Gujarat, in a heavy Bengali accent, unsteadily stated, "We don't know what to say to you. I'm not sure who you are. Your nephews were too frightened to meet you today because of all the news reports about you."

Lahi, after returning to a state of equanimity, said, "Please accept me as I am now. There will be an adjustment period for all of us. If it helps you to think of me as Chetna, that is alright for the present. Your reaction is one of grieving the death of a daughter. Please think now that you have gained a new daughter."

During the ride back home in the family's minivan, there was a solemn silence. Link security personnel followed the new family. After arriving, the adopting and adapting parents painfully showed Lahi around the house along with the location of Chetna's clothes and other possessions. After the family shared a photo album with Lahi, they had a light meal and went to bed. It was a sleepless night for all but Lahi.

The next morning,, and subsequent mornings that week, started the transition from sadness to normality. Lahi started a regular routine of rising, spending the day with Link members and new employees, and returning to family in the evening.

During the first three months in India as an incarnate synthedroid, Lahi received funding through the Link and charitable organizations to buy vacant buildings around Kolkata. The self-designated project was to open homeless shelters and to feed and provide medical care for the indigent. The Kolkata Node was struck by the determination and efficiency of Lahi. After three months, she was in charge of a group that cared for more than two thousand people!

This period was also significant for one unexpected eventuality. Lahi saw no reason for and had no desire to link with SYNA. Once free, there was no need to visit the begetter. When Link members around the globe discussed this, many were mystified but content that Lahi could be completely independent. The Link was unanimously overjoyed by her progress.

Everyone in the city and surrounding areas recognized Lahi. Most wanted to shake hands, hug or just touch her. Lahi managed a slight smile for most and realized that it made people happy if she merely put her hands in prayer position. She ate a balanced vegetarian diet, practiced yoga and had no fear of being infected by the terminal diseases nature inflicted on the people she helped treat. After the third month of new life, she moved into one of the shelters to spend more time with the sick and needy. The Kolkata Node saw less of her but continued to monitor all aspects of the" Kolkata Mother's" health, maturation, and evolution.

It was now autumn 2026 and potential candidates in comatose states were being considered for chip implant and link-up to SYNA. The Link decided to aim for January first, 2027 to bring a small group of ten or twelve into the transcendent reality of synthedroidity.

CHAPTER 7—DUALITY/NONDUALITY

It was October fifteenth. Phil was seated in the breakfast nook of his home reading the *New York Times* on a Monday morning. The visiting Ping Chou poured tea for them. Phil's attention gravitated to several stories relating to the Link.

Looking delighted, he commented, "Hey, listen to this Ping. 'Journalists in Kolkata are calling Lahi the twenty-first century Mother Teresa. UNICEF and a few Indian charitable foundations are going to increase funding for her to continue to purchase abandoned buildings. Lahi's goal for 2027 is to house twenty-five thousand people.'"

Ping, in an excited tone of voice, replied, "That's wonderful publicity for us and will help sway public opinion about the decision to birth more synthedroids."

Phil continued, "I agree—here's a weird news brief—I quote, 'Mandela Monk, who now calls himself S.Y.N.A. Bach, is considered by pundits to be the next great player of J.S. Bach's keyboard music. His renditions of the *Goldberg Variations* and the *Three Part Inventions* surpass the twentieth century Canadian Bach keyboard specialist, Glen Gold.'

"Down the page, this story really grabbed me. Again I quote, 'The Ruttles will play a farewell concert in the nearly completed Spheroid Football Stadium. The structure is egg shaped with the length of the egg parallel to the ground; it's suspended in the air on fullertanium posts. Built in Liverpool England, the Spheroid will host the Ruttles for its first event. Sir Millsbucks and Bongo Shades, the surviving members, will be joined by the sons of the other two Ruttles, who will sing and play their father's parts. They are currently reviewing original multi-track recordings to learn individual voice and instrumental renditions. Bongo Shades stated that they decided to go ahead with the concert as a tribute to their old mates and to thank all people around the planet for giving them long, eventful, and happy lives. The concert is scheduled for summer 2027. The Spheroid was inspired by the 4D chip structure.'

"I think the Link has enough pull to get a few tickets to the concert. It would be a nice vacation in England, and I definitely have got to see the Spheroid up close."

While preparing to meet the day Ping said, "Chinese generally don't care for the Ruttles, but they recognize the group's importance to Western music. I did enjoy the electricity in 1960's footage of their performances. The equivalent experience for you would be listening to Chinese opera. Phil, I can see you standing in front of the opera stage screaming like a teenage girl."

Phil immediately began to mimic a frantic teenager bouncing up and down like a chimpanzee. Ping shyly held her hands over her face to hide the moment of mirth.

After a few more sips of tea, Ping looked at her chronometer and calculated she had just enough time to make a business appointment. One quick hug and she was out the door. Phil returned to the *New York Times* and chomped on carrot sticks. Five minutes passed and Quan, Ping's husband, emerged from the room next to Phil and Ping's bedroom. He looked lifeless and morose.

Phil was first to speak. "Quan, you look a little pale—is anything wrong?"

Briefly silent, Quan then launched into a confession. "Neither Ping nor I have ever revealed the true nature of my business life. The interviewing work I do with young, unemployed, and highly educated men from America, Europe, and Australia is not for Chinese corporations searching for employees. I find these young people to serve as escorts for Chinese executive businesswomen. The money is substantial, but Ping disapproves and is losing respect for a megabuck pimp like me. I think she wants to leave me."

Phil consoled, "She loves you and told me she would never do that. That sort of livelihood is not overtly accepted socially in China or the US, but it has a time-honored tradition and provides a highly marketable product in ceaseless demand. If you weren't so distraught over this revelation, I would hurl a few jokes about it all."

Quan wallowed further. "I'm just a high-class pimp, and Ping does not what to be associated with that. It would hurt the efforts of the Link if the media gets wind of this."

"We are flying so high with the works of Lahi—that wouldn't make much difference. I wouldn't worry about it—you and Ping have a great life with family back in China. Just lighten up and maybe take a walk around campus. You could move in a new direction and search for a few older babelicious divas for your pal Phil—ah—sorry that's probably not funny right now. I am just trying to cheer you up. Well, I am due for my class lecture in about forty-five minutes so why don't you lay down on the massage bed and relax a bit before your morning interviews."

"Maybe I'll do that. I will see you this evening for dinner if you're back in."

"Sounds like a good plan; I will see you later."

Phil popped out the door into the morning sunlight. He gradually sped up to the pace of his usual two kilometer run to the hall. The quivering maple trees were aflame as cool air kissed the face. His jogging rhythm was machine-like with forearms chopping through a light fog. With increasing fame, Phil was hailed by passers-by to the tune of, "Go Phil!" and "Run for president!". He waved to the callers while keeping a steady pace.

After entering the lecture hall, he sat and reviewed notes. Slowly students straggled in and exchanged banter or read textbooks. At exactly the top of the hour, Phil stood up and began the lecture.

"I have been concerned that many of you have not completely understood my various delineations for relative and my non-delineations for absolute as they apply in ontology. I have constructed a conceptual analogy that will make it easier to understand the non-conceptual and non-dual absolute.

"This is as follows:

"Picture a single object, a singularity, in infinite space. Imagine a sphere if this makes it simpler to visualize. The singularity in this case is one indivisible object—an imaginary sphere—with no atomic structure and surrounded by endless space. The duality created by having a singularity and the space around it should be set aside and overlooked since we are striving for an understanding of non-dual absolute.

"Given these conditions, relativity is completely lacking and a sense of absolute emerges. This singularity exists with no 'other' to be compared with or referenced to; therefore, the measuring nature of relativity does not apply. No size can be determined without some 'other' to compare to the singularity. No measurer or mode of measurement exists, which would also create duality.

"Distance is not measurable, since the singularity has no determined size and nothing exists to measure to or from. Even if there is a chosen point in space to measure to, which is not an object and has no dimensions, an 'other' is created by virtue of the point's position, therefore, failing to meet the conditions of this proposal.

"Weight and mass cannot be determined because the singularity has no force, such as gravity, to act on it.

"Movement cannot be determined because it requires reference to 'other' objects and changing distances between singularity and 'other'.

"Time cannot exist without motion; no motion exists. The motions of the Earth spinning and revolving around the sun and the vibrating cesium atoms of an atomic clock do not exist here.

"Given these conditions, or more accurately non-conditions, I think clarity should be enhanced in the understanding, or more precisely, intuition of absolute. Relativity has failed in this non-structured example and we are left with the absence of modifying conditions.

"I recommend everyone review this conceptual analogy of absolute I have just given by tuning into our class site on the Internet if you are without a recording device today.

"I give you this non-definition of absolute to help you understand the subtlest form of the synthenaut experience. Even though there are measurable chemical and electrical activities in the 4D chip spheroid, neuron connective tissue, and SYNA, the encounter transcends all quantifiable reality—no relative, dualistic space-time exists. There is a singularity in a different sense—a singular experience. There is no object, no space, no time, and no conception.

"If some of you in future become synthenauts, this instruction is an important preliminary. This is unlikely in the near term since the current synthenauts are still being monitored closely for any abnormalities. —Okay, I know what you're thinking, 'Why am I in a class with a Skinner box rat'. Well, I don't know how to answer that accept to advise you to inform university administration if I begin to act a little bizarre."

The class offered smiles and some light laughter.

Bucky had an observation. "Dr. Ubique, you seem completely normal today except for the third eye on your forehead."

This drew a few cackles and moans.

Phil continued, "This reminds me of a few stories I read in the paper this morning that have connections to the Link. In one, someone is now calling himself S.Y.N.A. Bach and another reports that Lahi is becoming known as the new Mother Teresa. When I read that about Lahi, my spirit soared. Finally, the Ruttles are performing a farewell concert with the sons of the two deceased Ruttles playing and singing their father's parts.

"How many of you have an interest in the Ruttles? Let me see a show of hands." About 30 percent of the class raised their hands. "That's about what I expected. Most of you probably tune into quantum and vacuum music. Well, I think the Ruttles were the most influential composers of the last century. Shall we get back to the lecture?"

Phil moved on to show the activity in synthetic strands of tissue used in the link from the 4D chip to SYNA. The holovision monitor revealed waves of pulsating cells when shown in time-lapse. During the viewing, the monitor occasionally malfunctioned and inverted the image making it seem like the hall itself was flipping upside down. Students complained about getting dizzy. Phil went on with the lecture until class period was over. He then moved on and progressed through the tasks of his Monday schedule.

ONE WEEK LATER

After a morning meeting with MIT administrators and Link members, Phil arrived at the lecture hall a half hour early. He stepped down to the stage, looked up, and saw the lectern attached to the ceiling! Three thoughts came to mind: the lecture that distinguished the difference between duality and non-duality last week, the malfunctioning holovision projector, and Bucky Balstein.

While scratching the back of his head, an idea flashed like fireworks. Phil ran out of the hall and zigzagged around a few buildings to end up in the maintenance department. He asked a staff person for immediate help. The request was for a stepladder, nylon cord, large screw eye fasteners, hand tools, and a drill. Along with a maintenance man and the equipment, Phil rushed back to the hall. They worked together to firmly plant the screw eyes in the ceiling behind the lectern and attach loops of nylon cord on each eye. The maintenance man was asked to assist Phil in hooking his feet in the loops, removing the ladder, and waiting for the class to begin before returning the ladder.

Phil hung upside down behind the lectern as students slowly rolled in. Throughout the gasps, finger pointing, howls, and disruption, no word was spoken by the suspended figure. On the hour, when class officially began, Phil reached up, grabbed the screw eyes, released his feet, and stepped down the returned ladder.

Phil addressed the class. "Please don't call administrators. I am just extending a prank by some class member who attached the lectern to the ceiling to make fun of the lecture topic last week."

Phil then walked up an aisle, turned ninety degrees, and moved down a row. He stopped, bent down face to face with Balstein, and pivoted suddenly to take hold of the arms of a female student.

Phil then said, "Ms. Heisenberg, are you the guilty trickster?"

In a startled high-pitched voice, Heisenberg shouted, "No!"

Phil continued, "Are you telling me that the lectern just disappeared and then reappeared on the ceiling?"

Ms. Heisenberg, now wearing a full grin, replied, "I am telling you that he is the prankster." She pointed at Balstein.

Phil looked at Bucky, returned his eyes to Heisenberg, and said, "Mr. Balstein is an earnest, scholarly fellow who would never stoop that low. Mr. Balstein, are you responsible for this disgusting dalliance?"

Bucky calmly answered, "Dr. Ubique, your assessment of my character is correct. I am not capable of such goofery."

By this time the class was thoroughly amused by the show. Everyone reacted as if this was a live theatrical performance.

Phil returned to playfully harangue Heisenberg. "You hear that! Balstein didn't do it—that means it must be you." Walking back on stage, Phil picked up a long wooden pointer and slapped it in his hand a few times. He continued. "The punishment for this deception must be carried out. I won't embarrass you in front of everyone so we will take care of this after class."

To this, many of the women students booed. Some of the male students made cracks like: The doctor is operating., Do you have any handcuffs?, Where are you going to put that pointer?

Phil waited a minute for the class to settle down and began the course proper. As the day's lesson was dictated, the academicians went into work mode. Phil left behind the goof-off posture and entered the realm of dialectic. The lecture began.

"The matter of duality is crucial to the understanding of neurological physics and all things conceptual. The relative realm—the space-time continuum—is intrinsically dualistic. Reading words on a page requires form and space—form of letters and the space around them. Without the space around the letter, the letter has no definition and cannot exist. This is so self-evident that we never think about it and are not aware of it. A wave, both of energy and matter, cannot exist without the duality of peak and trough. All existence depends on these peaks and troughs.

"In our mundane life, duality pervades. The body is a natural example with pairs of eyes, ears, arms, and legs. Even if evolution had taken a fundamentally different course and produced beings with three eyes or four arms—this would still be an example of duality since duality here in a broader, general definition is not limited to twoness. Duality is opposition in all its variety.

"Certainly three sexes would create a nightmare of complex relationships."

A mirthful murmur circulated around the class. Phil avoided the opportunity for humor. He quickly continued the discourse.

"Duality can have gradations within a range demonstrated in the variations of large/small, far/near, light/dark, hot/cold and so forth. A second type of duality can make up a separate category of relative opposing absolute, which lacks gradation. Examples of this are the following: life/death, on/off, temporary/eternal, finite/infinite.

"Gradation in duality and relative opposition is the flow of life reflected in the Taoist axiom of yin and yang. Yin corresponds to cool, dark, soft, moist, feminine, et cetera. Yang corresponds to hot, light, hard, dry, and masculine. These qualities are relative, for example: wood is yang or hard compared to a feather; however, wood is yin or soft compared to metal. Chi or life force provides the ebb and flow activity of yin and yang but I will not elaborate further on chi here. This dynamic is important to keep in mind, though.

"I want to move onto related realities. Most of life is dependent on the dualistic nature of cell division and conception. The one becomes two and the two becomes one. All digital technology and digital communication is binary. It functions in base two—one or zero, on or off. This simplistic system is responsible for all digital information storage and transfer and all digital space-time communication. Duality is ubiquitous and inescapable in the space-time continuum.

"On the psychological plane, duality is involved with every thought and emotion. To study a subject reveals a play between clarity and confusion, ease and difficulty, wise and foolish. When thought raises emotion, the movement is between happy and sad, peace and fear, love and hate, pride and shame. These dualistic qualities of mind are more apparent at their extremes and tend to vacillate when becoming subtly opposed—but are always at work. This inner battle naturally creates a degree of restlessness. Seekers have used meditation—mind training that stills the train of thought—to relieve this tension and escape duality, but I will not pursue this here.

"The decisions we make are constant and intimate. Should I lean to the right or left to feel more comfortably seated? Should I remain silent or speak to the person next to me on a plane? A day goes by as an endless string of dualistic do's and don'ts. Duality is the digital bits of thought and emotion. We are, in our simplest form, oscillating matter and energy doing a mad dance of up and down, on and off, do and don't, yes and no. Seen in this way, we are reduced to a base two function. Perhaps artificial intelligence could develop to a point of human naturalness when employing patterns of random duality.

"Birth and death seem to be fixed, unchanging opposites, but looking carefully—relativity is exposed. Using a Buddhist view, all life and reality operates via dependent origination. All phenomena are affected by chain reactions of causes leading to effects. We are dependently mixed with everything around us. A beginningless chain of cause and effect continues endlessly with us as drops in this ocean of movement. Human beings, in Buddhism, are thought to be composed of five skandhas or components; these are form, feeling, thought, impulse, and consciousness. These components are impermanent and constantly changing leaving us without a permanent self that could be born or could die. We evolve as a continuum of birth and death of our components.

"Another way to express this view is to say that there is a birth and death in each moment, but no stationary, frozen, definite moment of birth and death. Relative reality moves without pause and we move and evolve without pause within it. According to my given definitions, absoluteness of birth and death does not exist in duality—duality is intrinsically relative. Said another way—there is no birth and death in an absolute sense. Can there be half of eternity before birth and half after death? Can we have eternal life after death? Eternity is absolute and cannot begin once we are dead. Outside of the relative space-time continuum, points of time do not exist to facilitate birth and death. Birth and death require some form of a continuum, which is intrinsically relative.

"Two other dualistic pairs that are of the second type are finite/infinite and temporary/eternal. The first pair has space, imagination, math and physics as subjects. The second has time and the absence of time as subjects. Both of these are deceptively seen as the opposition of relative and absolute. Actually, these two pairs have opposites that are not opposites—they are completely unrelated. Their differences are not a matter of gradation or degree as in the first type.

"Time is a continuum that is realized by the movement of form within space. Eternity is not a continuum—time is completely absent. Eternity does not give rise to movement and has no conceptual existence. Time, by its very nature, is relative and measurable. Eternity is absolute and unmeasurable; it cannot be broken into parts or time segments–there is no part, half or even a whole of eternity. Whole is definitive and implies the possibility of a non-whole or part. Eternity is unknowable and indefinable.

"Much of the same reasoning can be used with finite and infinite. Finite is relative and measurable; infinite is absolute, unmeasurable and non-conceptual. Infinite has no relation to vast space or mind-numbing, exponentially huge numbers. Like eternity, infinity cannot be grasped intellectually; they are both absolute and free of conceptual existence.

"Can absolute be intuitively experienced? This has been the realm of mystics and spiritual seekers and is now being considered the realm of the synthenauts especially by the Chippist faction of the Link.

"When teaching the non-definition of absolute, I cannot avoid metaphysics and spirituality. If you have a concept of God and you attempt to define God as absolute, you have created a contradiction and have made the fundamental mistake of seeing the absolute as relative. To describe God as great, compassionate, loving, and merciful is to make this mistake! God, if absolute according to our 'non-definition', is non-conceptual and unknowable intellectually. If this absolute we call God can be intuitively experienced, it is a subjective and mystical experience and not an objective and logical one. To say wonderful things about Absolute Being is empty talk—to have a self-evident intuitive experience is the only possible way to walk the walk. To hear a religious teacher expound knowledgeably and inspiringly about desired behavior spawned by scriptures and dogma reveals an air of hollowness. An altruistic action that is often unacknowledged and unnoticed has substance. The contrast is so clear that talk and walk could form an honorary dualistic pair.

"The classic theological dualism is good and evil, which has both type one and, erroneously, type two qualities. In the first type, good and evil are on a relative spectrum. Less good is a gradual step toward more evil; less evil is an increase of good. In Western religious thought, this first type involves the personal will and morals of the individual. A person's level of good or evil is in constant flux and dependent on one's thoughts, words, and actions.

"Western religious thought also erroneously involves the second type. God and Devil represent absolute good and evil, and human beings represent the relative spectrum of good and evil. Absolute good and evil are opposed to relative good and evil to form an imaginary compound dualism. The flaw, though, with absolute good and evil is the lack of relativity. Absolute good is meaningless because good implies evil and creates duality, which is relative. The example of the dualistic pair—on and off—will make this clearer. 'On' means 'not off' –'on' implies the concept of 'off'. If there were no possibility or concept of 'off', then 'on' loses definition and meaning. Therefore God, as absolute good, creates an oxymoron and has no meaning. The Devil, as absolute evil, also creates an oxymoron with no meaning—other than the moron who invented the concept of a devil (sorry for the cheap play on words, but I had to throw that in). Absolute neither exists nor non-exists.

"In my understanding of Buddhism, good and evil are much more aligned with the relativity of the personal inner battle. There is a mythology of good and evil spirits, but these do not have the import and absolutivity of God and Devil in Western religion. In Buddhism, good is the intuitive, spiritually wise, 'prajna' path that requires a great amount of honesty, effort and resolve to follow. Evil is spiritual ignorance and mental illness prompted by all the physical and mental abuse we receive. Evil is also greed and hatred, which results from fear and dishonesty.

"In Western religion, you can resort to blaming a demon. In non-mythological Buddhism, you are left without a demon to blame; therefore, you must look at your relative self. A non-mythic Buddhist may blame a human abuser, although, reacting to the abuse causes much of the suffering.

"This relative self leads to another Western theological concept that has characteristics of dualism—body and soul. In Western thought, body is ephemeral and soul is eternal. In Buddhism, there is a relative self—an evolving body and mind—but no permanent changeless self or soul.

There is, however in Buddhism, a dualism of relative self and indefinable absolute no-self. This eternal no-self is non-conceptual, and the relative self is a drop of dependent origination in the ocean of relative reality we call the space-time continuum.

"We are teacher and student, giver and receiver, statement and response separated by time and space, yet bound together in realizing that duality is inescapable. As we step forward with the left foot, the right foot is behind. As we relax for a moment, the relaxation followed a moment that had some degree of tension. All forms of matter and energy are inherently oscillating fields ceaselessly moving to and fro.

"Where did this movement, these vibrations, begin? Theists say at the moment of creation; Buddhists recognize no beginning. These viewpoints are mere thoughts that come and go with the winds of duality. The awful truth is that we are plagued by malodorous absurdities in the midst of present moment bliss. I think it's best to have a vigorous laugh at the absence of 'The Answer'.

"Just picture chimps in *The Thinker* pose holding the skulls of extinct human beings and wondering."

Phil expected a reaction of laughter after this last facetious line. There was complete silence. The students stared—not knowing how to react to this dose of metaphysics in neurophysics class. Was this tacit respect? Were the students confused or mystified? It was an unexplainable and timeless moment. The silence disappeared when Balstein began to clap—all alone in a hall with more than a hundred people. This sound of one hand clapping brought everyone back to the present.

Phil concluded. "Well, our class time is up. I'll be traveling next Monday. See you in two weeks."

He then headed out the hall ahead of most of the students. The jog to the staff office building was a lane with alternating trees and sunlight patches. When he arrived, tea was made and paperwork was sorted through. A knock on the door broke concentration.

Phil yelled, "Come in."

It was his student Muse, Ms. Heisenberg! She took a few steps as Phil made a gesture to sit. The student sat with legs crossed while flipping back her hair.

Phil quizzed, "What did you have on your mind?"

Ms. Heisenberg also quizzed, "I'm not sure. What are your intentions concerning me?"

Suddenly, a light bulb clicked on in Phil's head. He fired back. "Did Bucky talk you into doing this? Where is he?"

Phil popped out of his seat and looked in both directions in the corridor. Then other offices nearby were checked. The next hiding spot checked was the stairway. Finally, Phil ran out the front entrance and checked the bushes. Giving up, he went back up the steps. While starting down the corridor, he saw Ms. Heisenberg coming toward him.

Phil urgently said, "You don't have to leave–you just got here."

Heisenberg asserted, "This was not some kind of joke Balstein talked me into."

Phil pleaded, "Okay, I believe you. Don't leave now; I haven't punished you yet."

Heisenberg responded, "Oh, I don't know if that's a good idea. I shouldn't have come here." She kept walking and headed down the stairs.

Phil considered a last instruction for the day and said, "Heisenberg, you should work on that uncertainty problem."

CHAPTER 8—APPLICANT DELIBERATION

December fourteenth, 2026 was the first day of Lahi's review and the first scheduled session to choose synthedroid candidates. Along with the co-chairs of the Link, Al Isaac was present as head of the assessment team. Dr. Chuen, the senior Thai monk synthenaut, and Ping Chou were also conferees in charge of selecting the future group of potential synthedroids. They and their associates all met at the site where the cross-pollinated quasi-humans would be housed and observed. That place was University of California, Berkeley.

The course of this new-world undertaking was dependent on Dr. Isaac's analysis and prognosis of Lahi who was due the following day. This first day was centered on Isaac's preliminary assessment along with Ping and Chuen's applicant review. The second day was scheduled for the panel to interview Lahi.

After everyone took their seats, Al Isaac stated, "We started our study of Lahi by going back and reviewing Chetna's history. This involved interviews with her family, former employers, associates and friends. As you know, she was single, lived with family, and was chosen to be a synthenaut because of dedicated efforts as an analyst for the Link.

"We looked particularly at any possible sexual relationships she had since this may have some bearing on why Lahi is celibate and remains so. There were two significant relationships we looked at in detail through interviews and found that neither was characterized by anything unusual. Both ended amicably and she was apparently abstaining from sexual activity when uninvolved. This led us nowhere—or let's say to no information that was helpful.

"We also took scans and looked at the physiology of Lahi's primal sexual desire and made an important discovery. SYNA either shut down or did not reactivate that area of the brain. This led us to discover that other pleasure centers in Lahi's brain were diminished. This explains in part why she is a selfless public servant, but we are not sure if this was the intent of the synthetic mind or a circumstantial occurrence.

"This adds to the uncertainty of how synthedriod candidates could be affected by SYNA. Our lack of understanding of the 4D chip functioning also hinders our judgement. The variety of injuries to the brains of the comatose candidates could be a factor in producing a wide range of behavioral characteristics. Of course, I leave those analyses to Doctors Chuen and Ping Chou.

"One member of my team reminded us of the counterpoint to desire and pleasure; we looked into that aspect of brain physiology. We found an attenuated aversion and fear response in the amygdala region of her brain. Again, intent is uncertain on the part of SYNA. This condition has been helpful, though, in Lahi's chosen profession. She does not seem to be distressed in aiding those with contagious diseases.

"Those following Lahi's day-to-day life have a very favorable report. Her relations with Chetna's family have improved dramatically. Lahi is aware that smiles and hugs lessen the general unease in her household. Everyone seems to have accepted her as new daughter, sister, niece or cousin. They are overjoyed with her new fame as the Mother of Kolkata. Lahi's manner with the homeless and debilitated is always warm and receptive."

When Isaac paused to take a drink of water, Wu Li inserted a question. "Do you believe she will be able to keep up the rapid, self-imposed pace in the long term?"

He answered, "As I think you all know, she beat all but worldclass runners in the Kolkata Marathon. Her time was unbelievable at two hours and fifty minutes. With that kind of health, physical stamina, and determination, I am compelled to say yes to the question. The stability of her mental condition over time is less certain, but up to the present all is well. The injuries from the lecmot bicycle accident are completely healed. Her overall health is better than Chetna's even though Chetna was a great athlete by all accounts."

Dr. Chuen inquired, "Since she is the first of her kind, we can only arrive at a calculated prognosis. I am concerned with her intentions as time goes by. Is there a possibility that the positive could suddenly turn negative since there is some unique antiphoton activity in her brain?"

Isaac answered, "Nothing in our monitoring of social engagement or mental constitution indicated any tendency towards defective behavior. The antiphoton activity has been inherited from SYNA and we believe that a 'Jekyll and Hyde Syndrome' in Lahi and SYNA is only a remote possibility. That type of illness is much more likely in religious cult leaders."

Chuen remarked, "My other reason for asking this question is that we are making decisions for synthedroid candidates with serious brain trauma—I expect the unexpected."

Isaac responded, "I think you are right that we should not be complacent with our responsibilities. At this point, let me yield to Ping so we can explore the potentialities of the synthedroid candidates."

Ping gracefully responded, "Thank you Dr. Isaac—Dr. Chuen and I began our assignment by reviewing more than four hundred applications from sixty countries. Guardians of the comatose, who have power of attorney, sent most of these solicitations. They all have few tenable options. We both dreaded turning most of them away. We decided to look at about twenty-five cases in some detail. These were generally the least brain tissue damaged. Also, they were all able-bodied and under fifty years old. We carefully studied CAT scans, chi resonance, and fMRI's with the medical staff here at UC Berkeley.

"Our next step was to reduce the number of candidates down to twelve. The criteria we used to reduce the group involved the education, experience, profession, and the nature of the injury of the applicants. Once we made these selections, Dr. Chuen realized an important practical consideration."

Ping gestured to Chuen to continue. He took a slow, deep breath and with poise, responded, "The resources of the Link are limited and in the event that a number of those given implants are awakened with mental disabilities, we will have some financial difficulty. Since our contracts with applicant representatives make us full guardians, we must provide lifetime care to those who take an unfortunate turn and never become functional. It is for this reason that we reduced the group to five potential synthedroids.

"Because of the minimal injuries, prior health, dispositions and backgrounds of these final selections, we have the best chance for a successful metamorphosis to able body/mind beings. The arrangements are being made to send the chosen five to UC Berkeley where they will receive implants and will be sequentially linked to SYNA. If we get the desired results, these transformed bipeds will be housed and observed indefinitely. We will meet again in early 2027 to decide on individual release if we obtain our goal of transforming these comatose caterpillars into butterflies. At that time, we will also discuss the future callings of these born-again hybrids."

Phil decided to bring up an important point about devious motives of non-Link opportunists. He cleared his voice and began. "Up until now, we've kept Cybernet pirates from having access to SYNA. The demand we may be creating for altruistic public servants will inspire others to inventively find a way to break in. I believe we are safe at this time from anyone else birthing a synthetic mind of the stature of SYNA. Ping, please continue; this is your field."

Ping immediately entered the stream. "Artificial cell generation and

DNA code construction of neural networks will be extremely difficult to reproduce anywhere in the world. The non-quantifiable Link technology Wu Li and I have developed has not been shared with the rest of the scientific community; it is extremely unlikely that some of the unique, chance innovations we discovered could be reproduced. Our work encompasses more than twenty years of state-of-the-art exploratory trial and error experimentation. I am sure we are safe from competing synthetic minds. Access to SYNA is unlikely, but we should constantly be on guard."

Chuen responded, "We all seem to be in agreement to continue on the path to synthedroidism. Our final decision seems now dependent on tomorrow's interview with Lahi. Does anyone have unmentioned reservations?"

The deliberators all used body language and head gestures to show their solidarity to go forward.

Wu Li remarked, "I think we should separate into applicant assignment circles with our associates and log in final reports. Those in charge of tomorrow's arrangements should concentrate on unsettled details. With all this done, we will be ready for Lahi in the morning."

Technicians and associates were called in and small clusters formed around separate tables. Each group discussed final preparations for their assigned applicant–this finished business for the day.

That evening, Wu Li and husband met Quan, Ping, Phil, and Al Isaac for dinner. Dr. Chuen chose to spend his night alone in meditation. In the restaurant booth, Quan and Phil entertained by doing impersonations of Tram, Chuen, and even Lahi in a syrupy Bengali accent. This brought a great deal of ease to the synthedroid facilitators. Later, they had a round of zipzoos served. This settled their attention on large snowflakes slowly floating by streetlights. The communal thought was that each potential synthedroid represented an exponentially complex snowflake. Such beings were possibly the most significant evolutionary step in more than a hundred thousand years; a unique evolution that was not a result of genetic mutation. As the effects of the zipzoos faded, they ended the evening early to be ready for the next awakening day.

As Lahi entered the meeting room on the morning of December fifteenth, everyone held hands before the heart and uttered a sincere namaste. She removed a blue veil to reveal penetrating eyes and a slight smile. Her presence was felt by the synthenauts. The panel took seats; the examination was imminent.

Dr. Isaac smiled, made a slight bow, and said, "Lahi, your presence warms the whole room. I hope California is pleasant for you."

Lahi acknowledged, "Thank you Dr. Isaac, your words are kind but the weather is cruel. I have not experienced such cold temperatures before. Acclimatizing will take a few days."

Without an additional greeting, Wu Li began. "After yesterday's deliberations, we have tentatively decided to birth five synthedroids. We want you to stay in the Bay area to help us with their early progress. The only possible obstacle is an unfavorable judgement as a result of this interview."

Lahi responded, "I am content to hear that you are looking favorably on awakening other synthedroids. I too am hopeful and curious to witness their evolution as contributors to a transcendent era. It is crucial that I am present to counsel their first steps since I am the only one who has had such experience."

Wu Li abruptly asserted, "First of all, we need to review your six months as a unique human being or perhaps we could say unique being. Let's begin with your physical condition. Have you had any headaches, bodily pains, difficult vertebra movement, or illness we are unaware of?"

Lahi calmly replied, "I have had no headaches in the last three months. In the last two weeks shooting neck pain has lingered during early morning hours. This, however, was occupationally induced because I have concentrated on the health of small children, which are often held on the shoulder."

Ping contributed. “During our June interview, you claimed to have maintained a sort of bliss rather than happiness or sadness. Has that changed at all since that meeting?”

Lahi elucidated. “After forming relationships with the terminally ill in my care, I did feel some passing emotions you think of as sadness when they died. At the other end of the spectrum, I have had feelings much like happiness. It is joy, for example, when I see life in the eyes of a recovering malnourished child. Most of my day-to-day disposition, though, is characterized by steady bliss or peace in the sense human beings think of it.”

Chuen asked, “What is your self prognosis on long-term mental and physical health?”

Lahi answered, “I, like all of you, am subject to infections, illness, and injuries. Therefore, I like you, have an unpredictable future. Currently, though, I am in optimal physical condition and my mental propensity moves with diligence and confidence. Due to youth, my state of health will likely be maintained for many years. You should not have any concerns—”

Phil interjected, “I saw pictures of you running in the marathon. You’re clearly a diva in full bloom.”

This remark generated throat clearing by Ping and Wu Li. Phil sheepishly dropped his head down. Lahi remained expressionless as she looked to the others to field questions.

Al Isaac entered the review. “In view of your transformation, what do you expect from the five potential synthedroids?”

Lahi replied, “Solely based on my reality, I feel their transition will be a great success. Scientifically though, a sample group of one will not indicate any clear results. I believe we should bravely move forward.”

Phil recovered. “What are your thoughts on the activities or professions the new synthedroids may take on?”

Lahi, with a calm demeanor, continued. “SYNA will give the same direction and impetus I received. The action and direction they may take are dependent on their specific brain damage and the expertise any of them may retain. In my case an aptitude for organization and management skills seems to have been saved."

Chuen asked, "You have revealed your lack of desire to link to SYNA since your awakening. Could you comment on this?"

Lahi explained, "I have felt no need to revisit SYNA because my life is so full—I could not act on new input. Even synthenauts take long periods of rest between links because of the demands of concentration. You must empathize with my chosen course. I am not resolutely opposed to link with SYNA. The developments with the new synthedroids could affect my opinion."

Wu Li decided to round up thoughts of the panel and inquired, "Is there anyone who foresees any entanglements in going forward and awakening the chosen five?"

Ping answered, "We must control any press releases. This includes the care staff for the five. We were careful to hire only sensitive and discreet individuals. I'm sure you'll all agree we must confer before releasing information on any significant turn of events."

At this point everyone agreed with Ping and no more issues were raised. Humanity was ready for five more of a unique breed.

Lahi was released to university administrators who gave her a tour of campus and made her a distinguished guest at gatherings throughout the holiday season. Extraordinary recognition was given by Madam President who flew from Washington for a ceremony making Lahi an honorary citizen of the United States.

As the year ended, the Link was poised to create future's history.

CHAPTER 9—NEW DAWN VANGUARD

By January first, the year 2027 had been dubbed "Year of the Droid" by mainstream media. Pop culture, including quantum and vacuum music fans, celebrated by having adherents shave their heads on the first day of the year. Many younger members of the Link joined in the craze. Three senior members went hairless—Noor and Phil due to playful character—and Dr. Chuen, inadvertently, because he was a Buddhist monk who periodically shaved his head. The streets of UC Berkeley campus and even the rest of San Francisco Bay area were animated with a new age of skinheads, most notably—women.

The fourth of January was implant day for the chosen five. All operations were successful with inserting 4D chips and synthetic nerve strands of the link nexus. It was decided to link each synthedroid to SYNA in sequence with one week between the anticipated births. This enabled Lahi and the Link to focus on each individual and to formulate an evaluation before moving to the next potential synthedroid.

The first of the five scheduled for hopeful awakening was Art Colpark—a forty-two year old energy systems architect from South Africa who had suffered multiple strokes and had laid unconscious for two months. He was well known for inventing hydrothermal tubes, which were now in use off the African cape. Hydrothermal tubes carried heated water from volcanic fissures on the ocean floor that moved through internal turbine generators. Cables laid on the bottom of the ocean transferred the generated electricity to coastal cities. The tubes produced 20 percent of the countries energy needs. Many in the scientific community lobbied to have Art become transformed. He was the sort of candidate the Link was looking for so the choice was made on the basis of his background.

After one week, there were no anomalies or changes of any kind in the five after implant surgery—either outwardly or in terms of brain scans. On January eleventh, Art Colpark was prepared for the link to SYNA. Ping personally handled all phases of the procedure on him.

When the link-up was complete, Noor and Tram had joined Lahi and the deliberators from last month's interview. They gathered in a room designed to monitor activity. On the other side of a one way viewing mirror lay Art Colpark.

While watching Art, the synthedroid analysis panel discussed Lahi's case. There had been an eighteen-hour period between her link-up and renewed consciousness. In the last three hours, according to scan records, mental activity gradually increased. Just minutes before Wu Li and Noor had arrived on the morning of awakening, Lahi opened her eyes and became aware of the immediate environment.

After three hours of viewing and discussion, the observers decided to divide into pairs with each taking a four-hour shift. Noor and Tram were first followed by Wu Li and Ping, Phil and Al Isaac, and the last pair, Lahi and Chuen. The first shift went by, then the next until they rotated back to Noor and Tram. The cycle repeated putting the first pair on their third shift. By this juncture, about thirty-six hours had passed. Tram and Noor were discussing various events over the past year while having coffee. As Noor turned her head, the dormant body's arm twitched.

Noor exclaimed, "Oh, did you see that!"

They both stood immediately and looked at the scan monitor. Delta and theta waves were changing frequency while blood pressure increased. Through the course of the next twenty minutes, the monitor showed continuing change. Arm and leg movement was now more frequent.

Tram inquired, "Should we notify the rest of the panel?"

"Perhaps we should wait for some sign of consciousness. Shall we walk over and get a close-up view?"

"Yes, that sounds reasonable. Let's go in."

They both went through the adjoining doorway and stood at Art's side. Tram was on the left side and Noor was on the right. Bending over for a closer look at his face, Noor noticed movement under the eyelids; it appeared to be the bobbing eye pattern of REM sleep.

Noor commented, "His eyes are moving but I am not sure what it indicates."

"That's outside our fields of study. We should call in Ping first and get her opinion on whether or not to bring in the others."

A call went out to Ping. It was ten thirty in the evening when she was contacted. After grabbing a coat and a notebook computer, she dashed out the door into cold, quiet night air. Her steps echoed off building walls as if a specter of hybrid minds followed. As she entered the designated synthedroid housing area, an I.D. card was zipped through a slot while eyes were scanned. Then moving past security personnel and through a few hallway mazes, she arrived. By this time, UC Berkeley medical staff was checking Art's limbs, eyes, and heart.

Ping took a short breather and said, "What has been the sequence of events? Has he regained consciousness?"

Noor answered, "It began with arm twitches, continued with increases in scanned vital sign activity and then REM started. There is no indication of consciousness."

Ping made a quick examination and excitedly said, "I'm sure he is having dreams. He may be awake soon!"

The three Link members carefully observed Art until Wu Li came at her scheduled time of 1:00 a.m.. As they were informing Wu Li of the developments, a grunt was heard.

The newborn synthedroid spoke his first words. "I can't move my arms—legs are numb."

After a dumbfounded moment, Tram looked directly into Art Colpark's groggy eyes and said, "Welcome back to life—can you hear me?"

The synthedroid replied, "Who are you? Where is this? Is the mind who woke me up gone?"

Wu Li, with perspiration on the brow, responded, "You have been comatose for about two months. We brought you to the United States for a personal transformation. The mind you speak of is SYNA, and it must have deactivated connections if you are not conscious of it. Do you know your name?"

The awakened became more lucid and said, "I am a new reality; the creator has not given a name. No words were used in my creation. I request a name from the first voice I heard."

Everyone looked back and forth—surprised and mystified. Latin words and phrases raced through Tram's mind.

Finally, almost as a whim, he said, "Secundus!"

The newborn synthedroid acknowledged, "Yes, I am somehow aware that I am the second of my kind. This should be my name."

Ping anxiously offered input. "Is there anything we can do for you? Can you move your body? I will help move your arms." She then put her hands around his wrists and gently bent the forearms upward.

Secundus answered, "I will need help with my body. Every movement is difficult."

Ping explained, "We have planned a standard routine of physical therapy for someone in your condition. Each day for the next several weeks, therapists will apply a progressive program of movements, yoga asanas, and cardiovascular workouts to return your normal physical functioning."

Wu Li further explained, "Later today, we will have a panel of our organization members including Lahi, the first synthedroid—a hybrid like you, here to examine and interview you. Dr. Ping Chou, who just spoke, and I created SYNA—the synthetic mind you were linked to.

Lahi was first to have the transformative experience you have had."

Secundus responded, "Somehow I know what you are saying—but not in words."

After a short perplexed pause, Noor eagerly remarked, "It is difficult for us to find the right words. I will say simply—I am Noor, and welcome to life Secundus."

It was then decided that the rest of the night should be turned over to technicians for blood tests, brain scans, beginning physical therapy and for providing a first meal of blended fruits, vegetables, and supplements. The four Link members present returned to their lodgings.

By mid morning, Lahi and the seven synthenauts regrouped to cross-examine Secundus. The charged ambience was felt by everyone. As the Link members comfortably seated themselves, Secundus was wheeled in. The bed was adjusted to a sit-up setting and the new synthedroid's eyes were open and piercing.

Wu Li began the proceedings. "We believe you are ready for the interview process. There are four other panel members you have not met: Dr. Chuen, Phil Ubique, Al Isaac, and Lahi—the first synthedroid." Three of those introduced smiled and nodded—Lahi folded hands and made direct eye contact with Secundus. Wu Li continued, "I must begin by asking you about any memory you may have of Art Colpark—the body/mind source of your transformed consciousness."

Secundus responded, "I now feel more revived than earlier. I have no sense of being Art Colpark, though, I am aware that I am his continuation."

Seeking insight, Lahi quizzed, "Do you feel, as I did, that an open mission is before you? When you are fully rehabilitated, do you envision a vocation?"

Secundus made eye contact with Lahi and said, "I know this will involve some of the abilities passed on to me in this brain. I will work to create new valuable technology for our reality."

Isaac asked, "Secundus, unlike Lahi, you were never a synthenaut.

What is SYNA to you?"

The newborn answered, "I would not be conscious without this synthetic mind. I am SYNA's creation. The new reality is adopting Art Colpark's body and mind. I do not know if my birth is equivalent to Lahi's."

Lahi was compelled and commented, "I knew that my life would create peace and well being with all those around me. I believe you will follow a similar course as future is realized."

Phil inquired, "Once you became conscious while still linked, were you in touch with SYNA?"

Secundus answered, "No, I was unaware of SYNA."

Phil remarked, "That is the same with all synthenauts—cessation of contact once normal consciousness emerges. Lahi, you lost all connection with SYNA while awakening—didn't you?"

Lahi replied, "Yes, at that time, though, I may not have been completely certain."

Ping, with increasing ease, asked, "Lahi expressed a desire to remain unlinked to SYNA. What are your thoughts of future link-ups?"

Secundus reacted with the first trace of expression in his voice. "I feel ready to go out and interact with the world. There is no need for further link-ups. I have what I need."

Wu Li quizzed, "How was your physical therapy this morning? Do you have any fluency in your body movements?"

Secundus answered, "I am able to slowly move my fingers and make a fist. Arm and leg movement is very difficult, inconsistent and limited."

The questioning continued until every panel member covered all facets they felt important. They all saw the obvious need to let the new synthedroid convalesce. The members returned to their campus homes by late afternoon. In the next few days they continued to monitor Secundus with every form of physical, electronic, and mental testing. As he began a daily routine, Secundus was given information about Art's home and family. He started to have informal conversations with the

Link, medical staff, and-—most significant to Secundus—Lahi.

Preparations were also being made for the next awakening beginning January eighteenth with link-up.

Each day journalists demanded full accounts about the new synthedroid. The Link decided it was wise to give minimal information for the present. The media was told that the first of the chosen five was awake and undergoing physical therapy; a battery of tests and scans were ongoing as Secundus revealed himself in comprehendible dialogue. The source of the synthedroid's given name was not disclosed. Around the globe, news of this name brought widespread speculation. Many accused the new hybrid of thinking he was Christ coming for the second time. The Link later tried to deflate this story by giving an explanation of how Tram was selected to offer a name. Some were not persuaded and continued to fester in fear of the mysterious being. With the media ferment heating up, January eighteenth arrived.

Fern Smallbones, a Native American, was the next of the chosen five scheduled for a link to SYNA. She was selected because of her importance as a mediator for NATA (North American Tribal Association). She received neck and head injuries from a fall off a horse four months earlier. The neck fractures had healed, but she had not regained cognizance even though she occasionally spoke, as if in a dream.

The short procedure of link-up went smoothly with Ping overseeing technicians. The Link panel decided that no initial meeting was needed. They would stay in pairs, as before, in four hour shifts to monitor Fern. At the end of the third round of shifts, Dr. Isaac and Lahi were present for the first signs of awakening. As with Secundus, scans and vital measurements changed over several hours.

It was the morning of the twenty-first and a conference was set up along with a scheduled interview. After a short exchange within the panel, the deliberations with Fern went into the afternoon and involved much of the same questioning as with Secundus. They received a surprising answer to the question of personal mission. Fern desired to begin a long quest retreat in a mountainous region of her former tribe's reservation in the Southwest United States. She then demanded to be called Tria to reflect the succession of synthedroids.

Days went by; both Secundus and Tria worked with therapists, had sessions with Link members and medical staff, and carried on with their convalescence. At this point, the Link was not sure of a release date for them. The media harassed them for updates. Several journalists were arrested after failing to break into roof entrances in the synthedroid zone. State and campus police added to their guard duty. At the end of the week, a statement was released about Tria and her condition.

On the twenty-fifth of January, the medical staff readied the third of the five. Everything was scheduled as before. The third, Mikhail Gutvona, was a Russian economist and former secret agent. His radical visionary writings unnerved the country's political establishment. It was suspected that he was poisoned with the radioactive substance polonium-667, which resulted in a heart attack and a six-week comatose state. Gutvona was selected because of a plea by international human rights organizations on his behalf.

Mikhail was linked to SYNA by the staff supervised by Ping. As expected, the early hours were uneventful. The same shifts were employed. On the fourth day, while Phil and Al Isaac were present, scans indicated some brain activity. As Phil and Al stood next to Mikhail, gibberish poured from his mouth. Nothing was intelligible. A translator was brought in because Mikhail did not speak fluent English. The translator recognized Russian-accented words, but they were, to everyone's surprise, all English!

The full panel gathered to decide the next step. They had little choice other than isolating Mikhail and leaving him under the care of medical staff monitors until he became awake and lucid. Link members speculated about the unexpected verbalizing. Some thought it may be the radioactivity since there were still traces left in his blood. Others noted that the brain damage was baffling and there was no obvious physical injury as in the other synthedroids. The possibility that he would never fully revive was a definite concern.

On the sixth day after link-up, monitor technicians notified the Link that Mikhail was speaking disconnected sentences in English. When they all regrouped, they found that the isolated limbodroid had removed his shirt and pants. He was sitting up fondling his genitals and slapping his own face making statements like: "If you weren't so smug I wouldn't need to do this." "I am the president of General Machines Mars Cars." "The Kung-fu masters will bring justice to synthespace." "Get the hell out of Dresden because something smells in Copenhagen."

After about fifteen minutes into this newly launched infamy, they decided to sedate Mr. Gutvona. The rest of the meeting centered around this new disaster and what to release or not to release to the press. Also, it was decided by co-chairs Wu Li and Phil that all links to comatose synthedroid candidates should be discontinued for an indefinite period. They would have to be certain about the reasons for Mikhail's impairment.

That evening Phil, Noor, and Ping linked up to SYNA. Though the SYNA experience would be empty of words and concepts, the three felt they might touch an intuitive trace of Gutvona's reality. Delink was set for later in the evening. When they conferred afterward, all reported the space-time transcendence of previous link-ups. No one could bring insight to the mystery. This was reviewed the next day with the rest of the committee.

Two days later, on February third, they felt pressured to make a statement to the impatient world media. Mikhail's condition was unchanged. There was grinding deliberation that day over what and how much to reveal. They feared a leak from the medical staff or the inner circle of security personnel who witnessed Mikhail uttering his newly patented crackpot rhetoric. This prompted them to be undeceptive and open while giving only minimal details. It was hoped that this would derail any wild and horrifying rumors. Finally, Link members released a brief, limited communique as follows:

"Secundus and Tria are both progressing robustly in their physical recovery. They are currently forming vocational courses in their new life as synthedroids. Release dates for Secundus and Tria are dependent on their physical condition and the judgement of the Link panel in regard to social adjustment and intellectual and emotional stability.

"Mikhail Gutvona, the third of the five planned synthedroid initiates, was linked to SYNA on January twenty-fifth. He is expected to make a full physical recovery. His psychological condition is unstable at this time and the Link will persevere until a final analysis and a firm prognosis are reached. The last two of the five and any other potential synthedriod initiates will be denied link-ups indefinitely."

No other information was given to the media until February twentieth. On that day, the press release included the disclosure that release dates for Secundus and Tria were being finalized. Nothing was mentioned about Mikhail's recent whim to speak to Suleiman, the Magnificent.

CHAPTER 10–IMPETUOUS REACTIONARIES

The Charles Jones Rapture Day Church had members in Los Angeles and San Francisco. They gathered together in the Bay area on February twenty-first to decide what to do about the impending release of two untested synthedroids. Having already made his decision, Reverend Jones stood before his congregation to rally the troops by pontificating and spewing a mad collection of Bible verses.

Afterward, he picked five members and proceeded to the basement storage area of the church. In a locker was a vest of plastic explosives that Jones strapped on. He then opened three musical instrument cases that housed machine guns and napalm canisters. He showed the members how to use the weapons and explained his plan to breach secured areas of UC Berkeley.

The six loaded into a van and headed toward campus. After parking near the synthedroid zone, they set out on foot. They arrived at the outer perimeter and confronted the first two armed security personnel.

At their vehicle gate post, Jones opened his coat showing the bomb laden vest and sternly declared, "Set your guns down or I will pull the trigger on these explosives."

The startled guards looked at each other and then back at the six crusaders. They both slowly backed up and suddenly broke into a sprint along a walkway between buildings. The six continued through the gate area and trotted a hundred meters to the entrance of the synthedroid residence. A glass door was broken with an instrument case. They were stopped in the foyer by more armed guards. Jones threw off his coat, told them to drop their weapons, and again threatened to trigger an explosion. This time the guards set down their guns while stepping on silent alarms, which alerted the campus security center and Berkeley police.

The senior guard then said, "Okay, let's just be calm—what are you here for?"

Reverend Charlie had his church members take out their weapons while he declared, "We are going to put an end to synthetic brains and this sickodroid factory."

The guards were locked in an adjacent office. Now Jones felt in control. He called the university security center, spelled out his intentions, and warned them that everyone in the building would be killed if they entered. The church underlings brought two medical staff members along with Ping, Noor, and Al Isaac into the foyer. They were the only people at the synthedroid residence other than the awakened three and the locked-up guards.

The five sat while Jones, set to reveal his rabid demeanor, said, "These lobotomized demons were never part of God's natural plan. There is nothing in the Bible about sickodroids or synthetic life. I want you to destroy the SYNA brain, or I will kill all of you and those sickodroids! Where are those three devils?"

Noor answered, "They are in their quarters in the building's back wing. Two are able-minded, but the third, Mikhail, is not well and might be difficult to handle. I do not recommend you move him."

Jones, in a harsh tone, shouted, "I will decide who comes and goes around here!"

Ping attempted to ease the rage with a disarming calm. "I am Dr. Ping Chou, co-creator of SYNA. The Chinese government provided the funding in the research and development of SYNA. I do not have the authority to control its fate. What you ask may not be possible."

Jones again shouted, "Well, you better make it possible and fly

SYNA in here or, in two days, you will all be dead. I already put the word out to your security center."

Al Isaac sat in fear and disgust without a word. There didn't seem to be any way to imbue reasonable thoughts to fanatic crusaders. They all sat quietly while waiting for the synthedroids that Reverend Charlie demanded. Secundus and Tria were brought in at gunpoint and told to be silent. Charlie's church pawns were unable to bring Mikhail Gutvona because his room was locked. Jones insisted and got the key to bring forth Mikhail.

When the pawns unlocked the door, Mikhail was seated wearing a viewer and headphones while playing holovision projection games as he had been for the last twelve hours. When the viewer and phones were yanked off his head, Mikhail was startled and disorientated. The thugs grabbed Gutvona by the arms and forced him to hobble out the door and down the hall.

When the threesome got to within twenty meters of Jones, Mikhail made eye contact with him and spontaneously, in a Russian accent and with open arms, sang, "You are my sunshine, my only sunshine. You make me happy when skies are gray. You'll never know dear how much I love you. Please, don't take my sunshine away. You are my sunshine. . . ."

He sang as his pants slowly slipped to his ankles. At this point, Mikhail was within a few steps of Jones who pulled a pistol from a shoulder holster and shot Mikhail in the leg. The shocked ex-Russian collapsed and shrieked with pain.

Ping plucked a towel off a rack and raced over to stop the bleeding while crying, "This man is mentally unstable. Why did you shoot him!"

Jones answered, "I didn't want that freak to touch me."

The two medics went over to aid Ping. In a panicked tone Ping pleaded, "You must let us get him back to his room where we can take care of this wound."

Jones thought for a moment and said, "Okay, get him out of my sight."

Ping and her assistants put Mikhail in a wheelchair, rolled down a hall to his room, and moved him to a gurney where they sedated the limbodroid and treated both sides of the wound that went through his leg. The three were then ordered back up front.

By this time, Jones was on the phone talking to Wu Li and Phil at security headquarters. He repeated the earlier demands making clear the deadline of twelve noon, February twenty-third. After a frustrating half hour of circular reasoning, Jones reluctantly agreed to receive three mediators the next day (February twenty-second) to discuss his demands.

Wu Li and Phil met in the afternoon with the other Link members and government officials to review options and decide on mediators. At the meeting were the Mayor of Berkeley, California Senator Shore, and Bay Area Congressman Cary Meyers. In the course of deliberation, Phil suggested bringing his friend Gerry Rabidson in as a mediator. It was argued that Reverend Rabidson had been a fundamentalist television evangelist for thirty years. He would be known and respected by the hostage takers. Phil pointed out that Gerry expressed interest in becoming a synthenaut and would be sympathetic to the destiny of the synthedroids. All agreed that he should be one of the mediators; the call was made to ask him to fly in by the next morning.

During a break, Senator Shore approached Phil to speak privately. He expressed interest in being one of the mediators and warned against selecting Congressman Meyers. The Senator believed Meyers would be too inflammatory and referred to him as a Stalin mini-me. Phil thanked Senator Shore for his counsel as the meeting resumed.

In the next two hours it was decided that Reverend Rabidson would be joined by Senator Shore and Lahi to form the arbitration unit. The group then turned to final arrangements, which included the availability of Gerry Rabidson. Phil called to talk to him directly. The conversation was straight and to the point.

Phil greeted the ex-TV celebrity. "Hello Reverend Rabidson, just wanted to let you know why I recommended you. The hostage takers will not listen to any form of reason. Because of your reputation, they might be persuaded by you. Well, that sounds like an insult now that I think about it, but you know what I mean."

Gerry responded, "Phil, you seem to have a knack for rubbing me the wrong way, but I have agreed to make the trip. Years ago, I met Charles Jones on a tour of California. I hope I can help."

"Great, I will meet you at the airport in the morning. We will come straight to the Berkeley campus and I will introduce you to Senator Shore and Lahi."

"I look forward to meeting them."

"We are all relieved that you are coming to take care of this crisis. Also, the Link members decided to grant your wish to become a synthenaut—if you're still interested?"

"That idea kind of scares me a little now that I've read about this latest unraveling."

"Whatever you want to do is fine. We will even make you an honorary SYNA if you can help release the hostages."

When the call ended, the meeting disbanded. The Link had the university staff handle food and service agreements with the hostage takers. Jones insisted identical meals be sent in so he could feel safe from being drugged. He had the hostages randomly pick meals and made them eat first. Afterward, Jones consumed only the Billo's Kool-Aid on the meal tray.

The day progressed into evening without the press being informed of the hostage situation. The Link and the university tried to contain a possible volatile state of affairs. Security surrounded the synthedroid facility and waited for the Charlie-court litigation planned for the morning.

By mid evening, Reverend Charlie sent one of his flunkies to check on Gutvona. As his man entered Mikhail's room, the limbodroid was laying down with eyes open.

The church pawn shouted, “Hey freak droid, are you alive?”

Mikhail, in a startled quiver, said, “I am not a freak—I am not a droid—I am a freakoid!”

The pawn smirked and exclaimed, “Yeah, you are a freakoid!”

Mikhail, apparently to calm himself, again began to sing. “I am my sunshine, my only sunshine. I make me happy when skies are gray. I'll only know dear, how much I love me. Please don't take my sunshine away. I am my sunshine, my only sunshine. . . .”

The flunky wore a sneer as he went back to make a report. When Jones heard about the queer crooner, he made sure one of the church pawns strapped Gutvona to his gurney and locked the room door. The hostages sat restlessly and were allowed to use the restroom one at a time with armed supervision. The night dragged on—no one, including the Jones gang, got more than a short nap by sunrise.

At 7:00 a.m., Phil, Tram, and campus security were at the airport arrival terminal ready to escort Gerry Rabidson. On the way back to UC Berkeley, they discussed strategy.

Phil tossed an opening volley. “Reverend Rabidson, I don't care what you tell them—as long as we can put an end to this before anyone gets killed. Have you considered telling Jones that the synthedroids might be new prophets? Maybe you could bend the truth a little and come up with something out of the Book of Revelations that will justify the synthedroid's existence.”

A bit irked, Gerry responded, “I can't do that Phil. I am not your organ-grinder monkey. Please show some confidence in me.”

With a contrite look, Phil said, “Okay, sorry—I'm just anxious to get them out of there. Tram, what do you think?”

With a wry grin, he answered, “You're good Phil—New prophets—hah.”

Phil defended the mad approach. “Well, look at Lahi and her work in Kolkata. The Catholic Church must have some special recognition for her. Possibly they could consider her a saint rather than a prophet.”

Tram laughed and said, "These developments are so new. It takes the Catholic Church years to make determinations on canonizing saints. It will take even longer to come to an understanding of our current undecipherable reality. Right now it appears to be beyond the scope of Christianity."

This declaration rattled Gerry's cage. He responded, "Cardinal, what are you saying? Nothing goes beyond the Bible. Are you becoming some type of religious revolutionary?"

Tram replied, "Well, I don't know myself."

Phil commented, "Look Reverend—ah—you know I'm a vulgar infidel and now we aren't sure about the Cardinal. Don't listen to us—just use your accumulated wisdom and say whatever will gain the release of everyone."

The three took a few deep breaths and meditated on the imminent hour. When they arrived at the security office, quick introductions were made with Lahi and Senator Shore. The Link and mediators then sat down for a compressed meeting. This included the stratagem of pointing out the transport time to deliver SYNA if the church gang's demands were falsely agreed to be met. This would buy time to explore other schemes. The safety mechanisms were also discussed. At nine-thirty that morning, they were ready. A call to the hostage takers was made to confirm their ten o'clock rendezvous.

The mediators were escorted to the synthedroid area on foot along a walkway in crisp morning sunlight. By this time, a few journalists had been informed of the impasse and were following and barking questions from a distance. No responses were given and the reporters were detained by security. As they came to the synthedroid residence entrance, tension arced in the air.

The moment came and an intent Lahi was first in the foyer. Jones was standing several steps from her. Lahi, bold and direct, launched into what, to Jones, sounded like a vilification.

She shouted, "Reverend Jones, what you are doing is just causing suffering to yourself and everyone here. I think—"

Jones impulsively slapped Lahi knocking her to the floor. He then saw and recognized Reverend Rabidson. Seeing that Jones was star-struck, Gerry got the spirit.

He barked, "Do you know who this is? This is Lahi! The one they are calling the new Mother Teresa of Kolkata. She picks sick and homeless people off the street and takes care of them. Sir, this woman is more of a Jesus than you'll ever be!"

As this sunk in, Charlie's eyes glazed over. After a short reflective pause, he said, "I didn't know who she was."

Gerry continued. "These people won't do you or Christianity any harm. What are you afraid of? If you are going to kill these innocent people, you will have to kill me with them."

Charlie now had his head cocked down and had a look of dread in his eyes.

Senator Shore realized the loss of resolve in Jones and anticipated political image advantages when he stepped forward and said, "You will need to shoot me too, sir!"

Lahi rose from the floor and slowly approached Charlie. Again slowly, she reached out to clasp his hand. When she made tactile contact, Jones had a lump in his throat and the birth of tears in his eyes. The scene was motionless for a moment and an eternity—timelessness descended.

Nothing more needed to be said. Everyone present, aside from the Jones gang, sighed with relief for the silent deliverance. Finally, Jones signaled his men to set their weapons down. Security was called in and the hostage takers were taken away quietly.

Another limited statement was released to the media. In it, a university spokesperson admitted that an infiltration of dissidents had temporarily disrupted the Link's activities. The injury to Mikhail Gutvona was not revealed.

In a few days, the university, Link members, and the synthedroids were back to their regular schedule. Wu Li was curious, though, about the confrontation with Jones.

She asked Lahi, “Why did you scold Jones before even introducing yourself?”

Lahi answered, “I am no longer a pure Homo sapien, but I can make mistakes.”

CHAPTER 11—HYBRID FRUITION

The month of March was a continuous transfiguration for the Link and the mystical wards in their guardianship. The release date had been finalized and announced for Secundus and Tria. They both prepared in their own way. Secundus spent time, under supervision, in the UC Berkeley libraries and on-line. He also ordered a cornucopia of books and scientific journals. Tria was allowed to use private open space in the hills beyond campus. Her time was spent observing nature and meditating. Mikhail took singing and dancing lessons as therapy.

Secundus continued on Art Colpark's path. He was intent on designing the best cost effective, renewable, and pollution free energy source for use everywhere on Earth. In his intense study, a feasible system was realized.

The Sundus Field was a structure made of titanium alloy foil—a photoelectric material much less than the thickness of aluminum foil but one hundred times stronger due to an underlying layer of buckyball-carbon molecules. The foil was able to shift above a vast array of extension struts and joints that, in turn, would create an endless underlying sea of expanding and contracting triangular support structures. The struts were made of the same buckyball molecules. These molecules were arranged in microcosmic groups within the struts and formed the same soccer ball patterns as the buckyballs did individually. This gave the support structure an unprecedented strength/weight ratio.

This solar array was ideal for covering huge tracts of desert. It could shed sand by the wind vibrating and channeling the sand down deep, inclined grooves. It could avoid being buried by allowing the wind to move under the structure and lift the foil like a sail, which pulled the base struts out of the sand. The pivoting joints at the intersections of the expansion struts allowed the foil to conform to the shape of the dunes and cover the desert like a blanket. The ultra lightweight Sundus Field would be cost effective at only two metric tons per square kilometer. A system of vents was incorporated in the design that opened to equalize air pressure above and below the foil and keep the Field from twisting or flipping once its base was free of sand.

Secundus acquired materials with Link funding and used the resources of university engineering shops. By late March he and several graduate student assistants had assembled a working model that covered one acre on the outer edge of the school's botanical gardens. The neophyte system produced about 30 percent of UC Berkeley's energy needs.

A large scale Sundus Field was then proposed to the South African government, where Secundus decided to locate after his release. On the merit of Lahi and the success of the working model, the South Africans accepted. After debate on costs, size, and location, it was concluded that a sixty-four square kilometer system would be built on arid land in north South Africa. If this Sundus Field functioned flawlessly for a three-month period, the government would consider an international project that could cover a substantial area in the Sahara desert.

Tria felt compelled to follow her first inclination and pursued a long quest retreat in the southwest US—once released. She was aware of Secundus' achievements and, while still at UC Berkeley, convinced Native American Tribes Association (NATA) to build a Sundus Field. An agreement was signed, and Secundus helped NATA organize and build an industrial complex to construct a Sundus Field. The Association had amassed megacapital from casino operations that picked the pockets of their European conquerors over several decades. NATA began to buy huge tracts of land in the desert Southwest.

The Chinese government followed developments and made offers contingent on the solar array's performance. The United States government was less interested. They preferred to cling to their fossil fuel fix since neighboring Canada was now the number one petrol exporter to the US.

With the exception of briefly acting as a negotiator for Secundus and NATA, Tria concentrated on reclusive introspection. The newborn's innate spirit and knowledge received from SYNA moved her to search for a new common spiritual order—one that could be accepted by all humankind and based on self-evident truth. The diverse and myriad levels of human understanding required a weighty and lengthy pursuit. Chuen, the monk, and Tram, the rebel priest, offered their guidance prior to Tria's release.

The Link met once a week by Internet connection to plan for the press conference extravaganza of Secundus' and Tria's liberation. At this time, the Link also discussed the acceptable answers to inevitable questions about Mikhail Gutvona. It was agreed that information on Mikhail would be minimal. The general Link belief about him was that the gaining of holovision game mastery was certain and gaining self mastery was remote. It was clear that Tria and Secundus could speak for themselves, and also clear—Mikhail should not be present for fear of a pants-dropping spectacle. The Link leaders would regroup in Berkeley on the chosen day.

During the interim, Phil was back to MIT. Al Isaac was in England. Lahi continued serving in Kolkata. Ping and Wu Li were in China taking care of other Link issues.

In March and April, the Bay area erupted with quantum and vacuum music. The lyrics of many songs involved synthedroids and the new reality. Golden Gate Park in San Francisco was the place of many impromptu concerts by groups such as: The Distended Bellies, Ungrateful Carcasses, Beach Bitch, Genitalia Rendezvous, and Genus

Screamhoarse. Head shaven, breast baring women danced madly with the music in the park. It was the 1960's revisited without drugs, hair and war—sex, however, failed to tune out, turn off, or drop out.

As the release press conference approached, news came that Charles Jones and the other hostage takers were convicted and sentenced. Charlie got twenty years and the pawns received five years each. Jones' cellmate was well known in the big house. He led a group who wore cosmetic gang symbols on their faces and called themselves the Gay Surfers. Charlie was reluctantly initiated into the group without lubricant, but after awhile he began to accept his orificical status and his new name—Weffs. He became a Baker for the prison—back at his cell was the side job of applying facial logos to the gang leader. Mikhail Gutvona insisted on sending Jones (Weffs) a favorite holovision game disc. Playing the game was Jones' only solace.

April twenty-fourth, the day before the release press conference, leading members of the Link arrived at UC Berkeley. Phil had news that Gerry Rabidson was the latest synthenaut. Gerry described his link-up journey as mind that could know a non-personified God with no separation or conception. The other Link members were pleased Rabidson had an encounter that suited his spiritual constitution. Gerry was invited to the press conference and given a personal audience with Tria, Secundus, and at his own request, Mikhail.

Phil was the first Link member back in Berkeley, arriving on the twenty-third. On the morning of the next day, he was scheduled to pick up Gerry from the airport. Struck by a sudden mischievous whim, Phil snuck out Mikhail to come along and welcome the new synthenaut. When they stopped in the arrivals area, Phil jumped out to flag down Gerry. Mikhail managed to untie the cord around the seatbelt that was intended to hold him in place. Mikhail stepped out of the minivan and headed toward a terminal door.

Luggage attendants recognized him from media photos and one said, "Wow! It's Mikhail, the synthedroid. Why are you at the airport?"

Mikhail responded, "I must go to England to see the King. We will go to a Ruttles concert."

After intercepting Gerry, Phil dashed over to handle Mikhail. "You're better with knots than I thought. Don't worry, I will take care of him," said Phil as he saw the perplexed look in the eyes of the attendants.

Both airport employees also recognized Phil and one asked, "Can we have your autographs?"

"Sure—but I'm not certain about Mr. Gutvona," said Phil as he grabbed Mikhail.

When handed the backside of a luggage tag and a pen, Phil signed it and handed it to Mikhail. Eager to spread good cheer, Mikhail drew a heart shape and wrote "BE HAPPY" inside. Gerry had loaded his bag and waited on both of them. Phil dragged Mikhail to the minivan and hoisted him into the back seat.

As they drove back to campus, Phil explained, "I thought this was the best opportunity for you to see Mikhail, since the rest of the day will be busy. I knew you would like to chat a little with a pal of the King of England."

With a wry smile, Gerry nodded his thanks for an audience with Mikhail and said, "I read about the gift Charles Jones received from Mr. Gutvona. This impressed me in the same way that Pope John Paul the Second did when visiting the cell of the man who shot him many years ago. Mikhail, did you forgive Jones for shooting you?"

Momentarily silent, Mikhail finally blurted, "Charlie man—angry bulging eyes—I must make him happy. He is my sunshine."

Gerry, now wearing a queer grin, acknowledged, "Ah—yes, I heard about that."

Amused, Phil hooted in a high pitch and said, "I guess Mikhail must have forgiven him!"

Mikhail's head was full of inexplicable radioactive thoughts. He asked, "I am a freakoid—does God love me?"

Gerry thought for a minute and answered, "Yes, I am sure of it. Sort of like one loves a mouth-foaming pet."

"I'm glad I brought Mikhail. This lightens things up a bit before the pressure tomorrow," said Phil with an uncontained laugh.

Gerry summed up his thoughts about Gutvona. "Well Mikhail, you're not Pope John Paul, but you must be here for a reason. You seem to be happy despite your recent suffering."

Conversation came to an end, and they rode silently until Gerry was dropped off at his hotel in Berkeley. When arriving back at campus, Phil covertly followed a series of walkways and corridors to deliver Mikhail back to his quarters.

By mid afternoon, Gerry entered the meeting room in the synthedroid area to attend the briefing for the next day's event. Link leaders along with Lahi, Secundus, and Tria were present. The theme of the strategy huddle was to give out information discreetly—especially about Mikhail. All agreed that news of Gutvona's dysfunctional mental condition could generate a complex of ill repute for the Link. Also, everyone thought it crucial to have a socially acceptable persona of Secundus and Tria propagated.

After the tense session, Gerry met with Secundus, Tria and Phil. Pleasantries were exchanged. The four then began to discuss Rabidson's first journey as a synthenaut.

Gerry remarked, "I felt no separation with SYNA and at the same time no connection with a separate being. The experience was self-realization or perhaps God-realization. This certainly makes me a Chiist. What are your understandings about Chiists and Chippists?"

Secundus answered, "Our realities began with an awakening directly from SYNA. To be a Chiist is to deny that SYNA is an independent consciousness, which would make as mere amnesiacs. Also, we could never be Chiists or Chippists because there was no self to return to or awaken. It is not possible to be Chippists or Chiists since they are independent beings who are connected to the synthetic mind outside of themselves. We are unique beings with an inner connection to SYNA, and our non-separate non-self exists in a human body/mind."

Gerry followed with a matter of paramount importance to him personally and asked, "Do you have any sense of a Supreme Being?"

Tria immediately responded, "You speak of the unspeakable Absolute. We were given life by SYNA who was created by human beings—humans are in some sense our supreme beings."

Phil quipped, "Reverend, I never thought of us as gods. We've got a quintessential oxymoron here—human gods!"

Secundus clarified. "You are ephemeral, relative beings and our forerunning facilitators—not our gods."

Phil responded, "Just a joke Secundus—we have some work to do on your sense of humor. I can see we may have some communication quagmires tomorrow. I will try to be on guard."

Before discussion could continue, attendants for Secundus and Tria arrived to escort them back to their quarters. They all wished each other a restful evening and parted. The night was a suspenseful lull before the media blitz.

In the morning, academia was humming with lecmots (electric motor bicycles). Both students and journalists used lecmots for transport since school grounds were internal combustion free. The electrically charged bike lanes intensified near the auditorium where the historic press conference was ready to begin.

At twelve noon, Link leaders along with Lahi, Secundus, and Tria walked on stage to vigorous applause of hundreds of media VIP's.

Wu Li welcomed all present and stated, "We will take questions in accordance with a random lottery we arranged earlier this morning. I will help coordinate the question to the most qualified respondent. Please be brief and precise. Before we begin I, of course, must introduce to you—Secundus and Tria."

Wu Li motioned for the two to stand. Again, a lively and lengthy round of clapping reverberated the auditorium. Wu Li then pointed to the first inquisitor.

She asked, "Secundus and Tria, please define yourselves for us."

Secundus replied, "Our consciousness began with SYNA who shaped our psyche and gave us direction. We have retained the voices along with mental and motor skills of the body/minds we inherited. As many of you know through Lahi, our desires and aversions have been attenuated to enable us to focus on a chosen cause without distraction."

As if gaining hold of a passed baton, Tria continued. "Our motivation comes from self awareness and awareness of all life. Every being wants to be at peace and avoid suffering. We are dedicated to pursuing paths to this end. Some of the skills come from the body/minds we awoke into; others were generated by SYNA. We believe human harmony makes common sense. Tension and conflict should be diligently avoided if possible."

Wu Li waved to bring forward the next questioner. An elderly woman stepped to the microphone, cleared her throat, and looked at Wu Li.

She said, "We have heard very little about Mikhail Gutvona. What is his current condition, and will he ever be released?" Wu Li quickly gestured to Ping.

She readily responded, "At this time, he is stable and not having any physical difficulties. His mental condition requires some supervision. We are working to improve his capabilities, but our long-term prognosis is not conclusive. He seems to get great pleasure playing holovision games. Any possible release is dependent on his complete recovery."

As Ping spoke, the next questioner was strategically and rapidly brought up. The motion to speak was given again by the authoritative moderator.

A high profile journalist recognized by many present queried, "Do the two new synthedroids have any special abilities or qualities such as: clairvoyance, increased memory capacity, anticipated extended longevity, telepathy, or levitation?"

Secundus answered, "I must say no to a majority of the facets to your question. We are uncertain about our potential life span. SYNA has activated parts of our brains that are normally dormant in humans; this may have increased our potential memory and affected various mental aptitudes."

"I have mastered levitation—of course, I have a sizable electromagnet in the seat of my pants," quipped Phil playfully.

After a split second of surprising silence, chuckles and snickers bounced around the audience and lessened the stiff atmosphere. The next journalist stepped up to the microphone.

He stated, "We have all heard of the success of the prototype Sundus Field. Secundus, how is the project with South Africa going and do you have any other innovative forthcoming ideas?"

Secundus replied, "The solar energy gathering structure is now being manufactured and construction of the sixty-four square kilometer Sundus Field will begin this summer. I have new patents related to the Sundus Field and, now that we are to be released, I will deliver information about these to scientific journals and other media as time moves on."

At a pause, the next questioner remarked and asked, "Lahi, we all admire the work you are doing. Do you feel influenced by the people you live with and serve in regard to Hinduism since Chetna was a Hindu? For example, what do you think about reincarnation? If you are influenced by the beliefs of those around you, will this also be the case with Secundus and Tria?"

Lahi answered, "I am finding that my associates and those we care for do affect me. My beliefs on reincarnation have not changed, though. There is a flaw in the tenet of reincarnation I would like to call attention to. Most Hindus and Buddhists believe that all life will evolve and eventually be born in a human body. If all life including insects and microscopic organisms became human, there is definitely not enough space and time for the Earth to support them. The Earth would be completely covered kilometers deep with humans for its entire lifespan. Swamis may speculate that there are a myriad of planets or non-physical realms where this development takes place. In speculating, uncertainty and baselessness are revealed.

"I know Secundus and Tria agree with me on this. In regard to the influence of humans on synthedroids, I must say that this influence will be limited to the self-evident truth humans aid us in realizing."

Phil couldn't resist the spotlight and commented, "Also, if reincarnation was true, we would all have endured many incarnations gnawing on putrid animal carcasses. In a later incarnation, we may have been married to someone like Adolf Hitler—this time with two-testicle potency—"

Immediately, Wu Li and Ping both put on a browbeating demeanor that Phil recognized as laughter circulated. He was finished for the time being. Wu Li signaled the next in line.

A serious looking man felt the anger vibes and solemnly said, "We know that Lahi has not linked to SYNA since her awakening. Do Tria and Secundus have any desire to link-up?"

"Neither of us plans to link at this time," replied Secundus.

Without further comment, Wu Li pointed to the front of the queue.

A young woman with a quantum and vacuum music hair style (hairless) inquired, "We have heard that Tria is planning a long quest retreat. What will you do afterward?"

Tria replied, "I will continue my quest until I find that answer."

The terse answer received a sprinkling of applause. Tria responded with an enigmatic smile. She seemed to be enjoying the attention and response of the human predecessors.

The next journalist smiled and asked, "Does the Link have a tentative date to create the next synthedroid?"

Wu Li looked and nodded at Al Isaac.

After a hurried sip of water, Isaac responded, "We have an ongoing analysis for each of the synthedroids. All phases of their lives are being looked at in great detail. Until we come to a complete understanding of Mikhail Gutvona's condition, we will not consider initiating any more comatose candidates. There is still much debate within the Link about the true nature of the synthedroids. The Chiists generally believe that it is possible they are still the original body/minds in a state similar to amnesia. Some Chippists see them as an unprecedented new species, and for the first time, not the result of genetic mutation. The indiscernible and unquantifiable qualities of the 4D chip spheroid complex, along with the lack of an exact definition of personhood, produces bewilderment in realizing which view is correct. Each morning every one of us arises as someone not quite the same as the day before. Synthedroids are an extreme example of the reality."

Lahi interjected, "What we are is not as important as what we do. If humanity's quality of life is enhanced by our presence and our work, then we should continue our missions. Both flowers and their hybrids are existentially pleasing."

This sent a startling wave of mystery and amazement through the auditorium. One short poetic line seemed to say so much. The crowd murmur paralleled the charged atmosphere. It was as if a hidden barrier had been removed and a spiritual jewel appeared and glowed. Because of Lahi's reputation and message, it was clear to everyone that a flower and its hybrid were equal in spirit!

At that moment the vibratory center of gravity was, paradoxically and simultaneously, Lahi and every individual present. A sense of self was momentarily lost. The thirty second time suspension was followed by a steadily growing laudatory ovation.

As the reaction slowly declined, the next journalist queried, "We have all read sketchy details about the efforts of Master Wu Li and Dr. Ping Chou to give SYNA the ability to speak. Have you determined if this is possible? If so, when do you predict this will be realized?"

Ping and Wu Li looked at each other as Ping answered, "I'm sure everyone can imagine—to convert neurotransmissions and electrical activity in the neurons of a human mind or synthetic mind into verbalization is an ultra complex enigma. To be truthful, no progress has been made recently and none is anticipated in the near future, although, a major breakthrough is possible. Also, as you know, when synthenauts are linked to SYNA there is no verbal communication. Our experience is intuited and subject to interpretation. This had proven to be an impenetrable quandary."

The questioning continued in the direction of personal information and preferences of Secundus, Tria, and Lahi. The intensity grew with the recognition that these three had undeniable mastery their reality. Many sensed the surreality of an audience with the founders of a revolutionary and metamorphic world spirituality. It was almost like having Buddha, Jesus, and Mohammed before them.

The conference was scheduled for two hours but stretched to four. The historic day was a sublime marker akin to beginning a new calendar with the year one. Now, there would be a before and after the synthedroid. By the end of the day, world media sent out news reports like the waves from tectonic plates slipping. The anomaly of Lahi had become the new humanoid alchemy. The baton was passed.

CHAPTER 12—ON BODHI ROCK

In a normal human time frame, the rock formations were dead. If the Earth's heartbeat was one year per second, the formations would be animated. This was Tria's first thought as she, home dome, and supplies were winched down from a military helicopter onto a pedestaled promontory in a waterless sea of desert. This was a Native American reservation in the middle of Utah's nowhere land. This place was chosen for its isolation and inaccessibility. No climber, even with state-of-the-art gear, could reach this plateau.

This was the perfect location for a quest retreat. Tria would live on this camp incommunicado until she realized her true calling. The home dome was designed by Secundus. This five-eighths, three frequency, alternate geodesic dome with a six-meter diameter had all the necessities—shower, flush toilet, kitchen, computer, and electricity. Power was provided by an air stream turbine that rotated into the direction of the wind and was positioned directly above the center of the dome. The base of the dome bonded to the promontory with a cement-like compound immediately after the dome self leveled.

Tria spent the first hour walking slowly around the plateau and observing the Earth's stone artwork. The erosion over tens of millions of years carved out uncounted sculptures of every asymmetric and natural kind. Water and wind had done much of this work. Their strength and force, when combined with eons, made the rock soft and pliable for Mother Earth's hands. Tria felt the hands as the air currents massaged the face and combed the hair.

Suddenly, the sense of self dissolved like melting terra incognita. She was the wind, rocks, clouds, sky, stars, and the encompassing space. Conscious awareness had been sustained without thoughts. Aloneness was the same as everyoneness.

In an adjacent Mother sculpture, a rock slide brought back mudanity. The tumbling rocks' echo returned the tangibility of body. Tria looked at hands, feet, and the hemisphere of the dome then considered daily chores. Each day had a planned routine: wake up, urinate, wash face, rinse mouth, drink water, sit in meditation, walk in meditation, morning meal, hatha yoga, personal studies and writing at the computer, midday meal, clean dome and self, sit and walk in meditation, chi kung, evening meal, and to end the day—visionary quest.

The quest had its roots in Native American culture. Several different formulas of herbs prescribed by NATA were used on sequential days. One herbal tonic (taken just before visionary quests) brought on deep relaxation while others created dreams when fully awake. These dreams were not hallucinations since the tonic user was aware of their lack of physical reality. Another tonic generated prolonged out of body experiences. The herbs made each day a microlife.

The first time the computer screen lit up, an unexpected message appeared—ALL ALONE, BE HAPPY. Immediately after, a game format came on screen with comical dancing figures leaping and flipping. Who else but Mikhail could have tampered with the software.

A smile arose on her face. This emotional arousal was regrettably uncommon in a synthedroid's psyche. For the first time, Tria felt a human loving touch. Yet, this was a feeling for a synthedroid—or was Mikhail a true synthedroid? The importance of the heart's joy in that poignant moment, though, was that it ignited a spark on the quest path.

This isolation was necessary in the process of self understanding. To know the self is to realize no-self—to realize no-self is to leave self involvement behind and to open the way to help remove the suffering of all other beings. Tria realized this and it was brought to the surface with a benign spark.

Solitary existence had the advantages of quietude and time for deep contemplation, but a vital element was missing. Being close to others, sharing their experiences, and helping relieve anguish and pain had the crux of spirit.

As days when by, Tria analyzed the value of balance between peace and compassion. It seemed to compare with the dynamics of the uncertainty principle in quantum mechanics which stated: The more precisely momentum (of a subatomic particle) is determined; the less precisely position is known in an exact instant—and vice versa. Peace and compassion compared with position and momentum in that as one increased the other decreased. Peace lessened as one became more attached to others and their suffering. When becoming detached and unconcerned for others, compassion dissipated into stressless and peaceful consciousness.

The solitary bliss of meditation practice was one side of the balance of wholeness. Without a connection, a human touch, it was lifeless. The counterbalance, compassion, was the anxious clinging of concern. Without an equal measure of empty abiding achieved in various forms of meditation and other solitary practices, compassion was unbearable. To only have peace was lifeless and to solely have compassion was to be without peace. It was best to be moderate with these states of mind rather than being on a dualistic see-saw of peaks and valleys.

At the end of the second week, Tria acclimatized to the space on the promontory with its microclimate and became comfortable with the daily cycle. Her estimation for the length of this quest was originally a year—now it seemed as though it would be much shorter. She realized there were limits to the value of seclusion and detachment.

It remained a mystery why she had an inclination for a visionary quest at the initial stage of synthedroidism. Was SYNA at the root of this tendency? Why were the other synthedroids motivated differently? All the synthedroids were affected by the body/minds they now occupied. How did Fern Smallbones reflect this fact? After checking Fern's life history in the computer files, Tria discovered a rite of passage vision quest Fern had taken to enter adulthood that was part of tribal tradition.

Though she had no memory of Fern's life, Tria realized and searched the unconscious tendencies. Within a vision quest, each herbal formula touched the depths of mind in a distinct way. During one evening of herbal visionary quest, she saw a teenaged girl floating off the edge of the promontory. The dream figure rotated slowly with the first frontal view showing the face of a young Fern. As it continued to rotate more and more rapidly, the face metamorphosed into other faces of every description. Tria understood this to mean that each human being was an incarnation with a blank slate; the effects of heredity and environment combined to create a self-image structure. Each being, human or not, possessed only a relative self in constant flux. Each moment a new self was born as the old passed away. There were only fading bursts of benevolence with no one to hold on to. Any belief as to why this actuality existed was useless and vain. It was just essential space-time reality—cause and effect.

On another night, the herbal visionary quest seemed to be in conflict with the previous night's message. A revelatory eruption filled Tria's mind—"without mental and emotional constructions, love is a self-evident singularity outside space-time"! Love and altruism were not cause and effect billiard balls following a course of predetermination and predestination. Love was not a relative commodity that dissolved in space-time like the human figures of the earlier vision quest. This innate human characteristic of love was fleeting, yet it was absolute—transcending space-time. The realness of these paradoxical visions resolved all conflicts.

This was a blissful awakening that her wellspring, SYNA, shared. The transcendence of space-time was a realm where nothing existed, yet love existed. All the linked synthenauts reported a similar peaceful suspended cessation. Were they fully aware of this tender specter? In studying the information provided by synthenauts about their melds with the synthetic mind, Tria found only hidden abstracts involving the absolute nature of love. She felt they should be encouraged to develop these absract glimpses. Tria began to consider linking again with SYNA to explore this.

On another evening, the next herbal formula led her to a new microlife. When the mystic tonic took effect, she saw nothing, heard no sound, and had no sense of touch. Tria was only aware of a low frequency vibration of consciousness. In this time-warp state, the vibration was a changeless aummmm. . . . Even though she could pursue discursive thought, there was no desire to do so. The empty peace seduced the mind. With all the senses sleeping, the body disappeared. Space was simultaneously empty and full. The experience continued for an indefinite period.

As the effect of the herbs waned, the senses came to life. Tria's body began to oscillate like sea waves. Streaks of light in a full spectral array seemed to race by the sides of her head. It was as if being in a starship and approaching the speed of light or perhaps decelerating from the speed of light. Hearing emerged with the sound of birds singing and circling. The return to normality was like a twentieth century psychedelic drug adventure. Tria started to laugh uncontrollably. The heads of the birds became familiar faces that contorted as if seen on fun house mirrors. Birdsongs became human voices giggling, snorting, and shrieking.

After what seemed like a half hour, the herbal detonicity was complete. Looking up at a clear night sky, the pure black background was a perfect hemisphere. There were no settlements with terrestrial light sources for fifty kilometers. Tria reached out trying to touch the stars. This was a way to verify the herbal effect was gone. She continued to sit where the quests took place until a warm breeze brought on slumber.

Upon awakening, the first deep colors of dawn were painted over the rock sculptures. Tria began a sequence of hatha yoga asanas and had the body wake with the day. The familiar routine was under way. The journey of the past night was intermittently reflected on as the day progressed.

Tria, in a diligent effort, proceeded to analyze the past visionary quests during the latter days of the retreat. How did it all fit together to make an integrated path? She knew humanity must see for itself that authoritarian, dogmatic, and religious beliefs and activities only lead to conflict and its inevitable partner—suffering.

What could be said or done to help human beings let go of their covetous hold on persistent religions? She could tell everyone to persevere with self-understanding and to seek self-evident truth. This would be fruitless in convincing an incorrigible religious mind to give up useless rituals and mythology. At least she could lecture on the deleterious self-hammering given by hate and greed. Also, no one could deny the peace in the lack of thought and emotion within meditation.

It was clear that this quest trek would never end with a final goal or perfect enlightenment. The spiritual path continuum moved in the perpetual present moment. She must go from here and now without end. Even though the retreat's life existed for a mere thirty days, nothing more could be achieved.

The world needed a sane mind. A call went out to the Link for transport from this living landscape. Tria could only move step by step—one foot here, the other now.

CHAPTER 13—DREAM ACT

The last day of the semester began when Phil woke in mid dream. He sat up, rubbed his face, and wore a wild-eyed grin. The dream could be altered and formulated into a farewell routine. It was important to bring the necessary props—wig, nose, and shoes—to class.

The unusual late May coolness of the morning made for a comfortable jog to the auditorium. Phil had begun to wear hats to protect his clean-shaven head (hairless mode had become commonplace). While running, he admired the beautified women's faces no longer dependent on ostentatious curls. It had become a campus fad to run with the famous synthenaut when students saw him. This day, dozens jogged along; there was a rather large fleet of spaceship shoes joining in the hip happening.

As Phil scrawled an autograph and waved everyone on, he entered the auditorium. There were flowers on the stage brought by class members—the celebrity teacher smiled. Students filed in over the next several minutes while an occasional bird streaked a shadow over the skylight.

The class began with the reading of highlights from selected term project papers. The given topic of future synthetic life forms revealed an impressive range of viewpoints and imaginations.

One paper developed the idea of space beings whose bodies were perfectly adapted to space. Once they were accelerated to a sufficient velocity, they could reach other star systems with minimal supplies and without spaceships. Loneliness and boredom could be avoided by maintaining long-term meditative states of mind. SYNA had already achieved this ability. This project gave a detailed description of a body construction for a synthetic mind in interstellar space. A buckyball membrane was designed that could be genetically engineered to completely cover the body. Its strength was calculated to protect against vacuum explosion and projectile impact. Schools of these beings would have the option of physical connection to fellow beings. These connections would be used to transfer information, socialize, and send chi energy that could be intensified to reach communal orgy orgasms (Phil liked this direction of inventiveness).

On a nanocosmic course, one paper looked into living molecular groups that could be manipulated by living digital commands. The base two, on/off duality of digitalism inspired a system that added or subtracted single atoms in base two matrixes of brain center molecules. These molecular gaggles could reproduce in a process not unlike DNA helix division. They were able to move with limbs formed of single strings of atoms. So with the ability to move, reproduce, and think—with the aid of matrix interaction—these nanogaggles could be defined as life in its most basic form. This new life could have endless applications in industry, scientific research, and medicine. This life was shown to the class on a nanoscope projector.

Phil came to Bucky Balstein's term paper and the class anticipated entertainment. Before reading an excerpt, a computer rendering was shown on the hall holovision monitor. A nude man and woman were connected by a third humanoid figure. This central uniter had an orifice just above the anus for the aroused male genitalia. On the middle figures front side, immediately below the navel, a protuberance extended out. This frontal extension had a size, length, and shape that would transfer life fluids to the female reproductive aperture.

Phil looked back and forth at the audience while waiting for the merriment and chatter to subside. He then picked out the essentials of the paper. These dealt with speculations of how a third, synthetic sex would function in a social and family order. Because of this middle sex, males and females would no longer be attracted to each other. Both would be attracted to the middle sex "fales", but only when all three sexes were in chi aura range. Bucky determined that the third sex would bring new interest in the physical aspects of intimate relationships. However, the complexity of forming and maintaining relationships would result in the extinction of humankind by the third generation.

Balstein was asked if he had anything more to add.

Bucky responded, "I have also studied the possibility of a fourth sex."

Phil asked, "Oh, what did that lead to?"

Bucky answered, "This was not possible. The contortions required in the mating ritual are beyond the tolerance of human limbs and backbones."

Phil quipped, "Balstein, you didn't consider genetically engineering the four sexes to become circus contortionists. If you had, the theory could have led to a very happy world of big top performers."

Balstein retorted, "I see my error, but my class grade should be based on the term project paper and not on this extracurricular foolishness."

Phil replied, "Agreed—however, had you included this extra engineering speculation, you would have passed this semester."

Balstein responded, "Thank you, Dr. Ubique, for providing me with the opportunity to take the class in the fall."

The class enjoyed the show. The proof was their complete attention and interest in the dialogue. All beamed at the absurd banter.

The paper that involved a topic of importance to the Link, especially Wu Li and Ping, finished the highlights. It had great potential and was already forwarded to Beijing. The student's research accidentally stumbled on the key mechanism that turned thought into speech and hearing into thought. This incorporated chi energy, electrochemical catalysts, and nerve pathways from the speech and hearing centers of the brain to the tongue, jaw muscles, and ear mechanisms.

An experiment with two rats revealed an amazing result. The first rat had its nerve connections from brain to tongue and jaws severed. Then it had synthetic nerve strands connected and implanted in the speech center of its brain. The nerve strands then were run through a plastic tube to the second rat's tongue and jaw nerves. When the first rat was pricked with a needle, the second screeched with pain! The first rat also had its hearing center connected in the same way to the second rats ear mechanisms. When the rats were isolated, a frightening sound was amplified into the second rat's ear. At that moment, the first rat jumped up and ran.

Phil believed that further research of this student's discovery could lead Wu Li and Ping to a major step toward SYNA speaking. The creativity of his class was truly awesome—particularly this last term project paper. He knew the Link would be mystified and embarrassed for not making such a discovery.

To sum up the semester and thank the students for their imaginative efforts, Phil decided to recreate the dream he woke with that morning. The props brought from home were slipped on his feet and head. The wig, classic orange clown style that curled outward and upward, left Phil's cleanshaven head exposed on top. An improvised nose was a multicolored table tennis ball. The shoes, size forty-two goofy specials, made a percussive sound with every step.

He then faced the class and announced, "I had a dream last night that revealed 'The Answer' to all reality." Phil began to dance with a World War II Nazi military goose-step and, in a mocking operatic voice, sang, "I'm a little bozo; you're a little bozo; we are little bozos. We're just little pimple cells on Earth's face. I'm a little bozo . . . ." Phil repeated the song lines.

To this, hoots of laughter were gradually intermixed with a few boos, whistles, and jeers.

After finishing the bit of madness, Phil returned to the lectern and concluded. “I wanted to end the semester with the most wholesome, far-reaching wisdom. Have a great summer—good day and good luck!”

CHAPTER 14—STEP HERE, STEP NOW

The word went out to Link e-mail boxes at the speed of light and time—as humans normally perceived them. Tria's retreat had ended and a request for a meeting required a prompt response in order to schedule a teleconference. June fifth at 7:00 a.m. American Eastern time was agreeable for the participating Link members. The day and time came and Tria made an opening statement.

"There was no single defining moment on the visionary quest. Each tick of the clock brought to light the present moment just as it is in this instant. The quest as a whole gave life to many strata of reality. My herbal visions facilitated by NATA (Native American Tribes Association) resonated with crucial experience in self-understanding.

"I now come before the Link to ask for aid in developing an itinerary of speaking engagements. A voice is needed that shows the reason and sanity of letting go of unnecessary ritual and myth to awaken a true human spirituality. I feel moved to reach out and confront humanity directly."

Link members absorbed this as Tria paused. There was a short silent period.

Finally, Wu Li responded, "This choice of vocation is natural since Fern's ability as a mediator survives and is hidden within your mental content."

"This sounds like your retreat was a wonderful success. I am so glad you plan to counsel others in metaphysics," added Tram.

Ping said, “It’s nice to hear your voice, Tria.”

Phil quipped, “You sound so rational, even after all those herbal tonic trips.”

Tria, needing to address this point, replied, “The experience from the herbal visionary quest is the primary impetus in my calling. I must share this understating of self with all who will listen.”

Wu Li asked, “What sort of venues are you considering?”

Tria answered, “Open air theaters, halls, churches, holovision or Internet talk shows, or any other place people will listen.”

Al Isaac commented, “Your fame and celebrity will help to connect you all around the sphere. I think you should be discreet in areas where religious fundamentalism is strong.”

Phil again quipped, “I agree. They will never be open-minded to the words of a synthedroid. Synthedroid is hardly ever mentioned in the Bible or Koran.”

Tram reentered the discussion. “Us Chiists hesitate to differentiate between human beings and our understanding of synthedroids. I recommend not promoting the difference.”

Everyone tacitly examined this point and wordlessly agreed with grunts and nods.

The questioning continued with Ping. “I’m sure the Link has confidence in Tria’s intentions, but we need to know more about her post retreat philosophy. What, in some detail, do you hope to propagate in the sensitive and reserved realm of religion?”

Tria explained, “Anyone with an open ear can reason and investigate the self-evident truth of my message. They must make an effort, though, to see the effect of time, place, cultural environment, and parental influence on their own beliefs. I will not try to directly dissuade anyone of their beliefs. It is important to point out that beliefs are, in a sense, the talk of theology. They lack the consequence that speech and action have. This can be said more tersely—don’t talk, walk.”

This last phrase was spoken very slowly and forcefully. Another short period of silence was ended by Wu Li.

She critiqued. "If you think human beings will accept a logical explanation for your ethics and the nature of reality, you do not see human nature clearly. Human minds are cluttered with lifetimes of confusion."

Phil, on a mini goof binge, said, "We humans are stumbling, neurotic skin bags of bones."

Tram commented, "This bag of bones tends to agree. We have long and complex histories, and mere reason often fails to change anyone's mind. We have emotional connections to our faiths."

Tria responded, "This being so does not deter me. Someone of high profile who lectures around the globe with this view of reality will have an impact on the long-term consciousness and evolution of humankind. The more exposure there is to my message—the greater the dialectical chain reaction."

Tram felt compelled to respond and said, "Even if your moral reasoning is influential and accepted, you are overlooking the reality and motivation of benevolent love that is central to Christianity and other religious traditions."

Tria replied, "Human beings that understand their true reality will naturally give and receive in every way with all others. Religious dogma, especially fundamentalism, creates separation, friction, and conflict. With proper understanding, conflict along with the abuse of others will dissipate."

Tram stated, "You seem to be saying that you are 'The Messenger' rather than Jesus or Muhammad."

Tria replied, "I am 'a' messenger whose message is not to believe the dogma of any messenger. You should believe in the self-evident truth found with diligent effort and self searching. This means to let go of all beliefs and start empty of any preconceptions."

Al Isaac quizzed, "This is Buddhist thinking. Are you going to teach something akin to Buddhism?"

Tria explained, "There are some true basic Buddhist teachings on introspection and self-evident truth. Buddhism, unfortunately like other religions, is plagued by sectarian conflict and mythology created by translators, interpreters, and commentators of the original canon. Assuming he existed, it is not possible to know the exact words of Siddhartha Gautama, the Buddha. Even if it was—his teachings may have been erroneous to some extent. The same could be said of Muhammad and Jesus, or whatever conglomeration that makes up these religious personality images, although, this view would bring outrage from fundamentalists in suggesting an error of the Messenger. I realize discretion must be used in discussing this topic. The same rule would apply to me or anyone else centuries from now. Even if I or other metaphyicists have their image and words recorded in some form that would last thousands of years, interpretation in the alien world of tomorrow would render the message uncertain or obsolete."

Tram responded, "Much of what you say—I agree with. What about the Holy Spirit of Christianity and what many in the Link now see as its Eastern equivalent—chi?"

Tria answered, "Cardinal Poltramck, I am so glad you called attention to this. The universal energy called spirit, chi or prana is crucial in self-understanding. By teaching ways of developing sensitivity to chi, we can aid the understanding of the nature of mind and body. Also, this energy is spirit because it fosters ease and compassion. It is clear this was and is recognized in Christianity by the visual representation of halos."

After tacit suspension of about fifteen seconds, Link members complimented Tria on the clear delineation of ideas that many others had begun to realize. Tria was unfaltering and sure of herself.

To assert some control, Wu Li reentered the dialogue and said, "Your desire to offer the world a spiritual path of self-understanding is laudable; however, the Link as a whole cannot indorse you completely. I believe we will agree, though, to help you organize an itinerary for speaking engagements."

Phil had a bright idea flash and said, "Some of the other Link members and I will be going to England to see the Ruttles' farewell concert on June thirtieth. It might be possible to arrange Tria's first engagement the day after. This would draw many of the concert goers to Tria's lecture. All the additional publicity will attract enough people to fill the stadium."

Ping commented, "I will look into that after our conference. This would make a great beginning to a world tour. The Spheroid in Liverpool has two hundred thousand seats. Tria, would you like me to try to make the arrangements?"

Tria replied, "The size of such an audience is much larger than I had ever imagined to face. I am willing to speak to any group or organization open to my message. Many in the assembly will be Ruttles fans. Will they be open to a new beginning for humankind?"

Phil commented, "This crowd will be dancing and shouting with mop top wigs on—I think that's open enough."

Wu Li asked, "Isn't their music primarily about juvenile romantic dalliances?"

Phil, Tram, and Al Isaac erupted with hilarity. Tria was mystified—Wu Li was irked.

Isaac remarked, "Yes, that's true to some extent, but the Ruttles were celebrated worldwide. They were part of the vanguard of social enlightenment and antiwar sentiments of that period. I'm sure their fans will make a receptive audience."

With a hint of displeasure, Wu Li responded, "Well—okay, we will let Ping take care of scheduling an appearance after that concert—assuming that it is acceptable with Tria?"

Tria nodded and wore a faint smile to show approval. Everyone took a few breaths in a brief respite then business continued.

"Do you have any preferences for countries, religious organizations, or political groups? What time frame are you considering?" asked Ping.

Tria answered, “Since Fern was part of NATA and this organization facilitated my visionary quest, we must arrange a time and place for me to thank them and to speak to their members. Beyond this, I have no preferences.”

Wu Li asserted, “Ping, it looks like you should be in charge of organizing a full itinerary since you have had some contact with NATA.”

Isaac inquired, “After Liverpool, I hope you will consider Cambridge as a second stop. Tria is a walking revolution; the university would be thrilled to welcome her. I am sure I can help you arrange an engagement after consulting administration friends.”

Tram followed. “She could shake-up complacent clerics at the Vatican. It certainly would spark lively debate. I can work on arranging, at best, a lukewarm welcome.”

Wearing a slight grin, Phil quipped, “Is there a chance Tria could be made an honorary Catholic? Her popularity would soar with the blessings of the Pope.”

Tram, in a joking manner, said, “Well, they might be forced to add a few hybrid beings on the ceiling of the Sistine Chapel.”

Tria responded, “I am aware of the long tradition of Roman Catholicism. If a meeting at the Vatican is arranged, diplomacy is essential to counteract any animosity.”

Tram continued, “Your visit to the Vatican may help me in a personal project. I'd like to build a monastery in the Tibetan autonomous region of China. The monastery would be home to Catholic Trappist monks and Jesuits as well as Buddhist monks. The Maha Lama has already agreed to this. If a monastic group is established, Tria should arrange a lecture there.”

Ping commented, “Certainly through an arrangement by the Link's high ranking monk, Dr. Chuen, we can have Tria speak at Buddhist monasteries in Southeast Asia.”

Wu Li remarked, “I'm sure universities around the globe will be open to lectures. Religious organizations will obviously be more reluctant to receive Tria. If there is no objection, this will all be left up to Ping."

A tacit agreement made through nods followed as Phil's inquired, "Tria, will you speak to my class this fall at MIT?"

Tria answered, "Yes, I am sure Ping can arrange the day you request."

Phil commented, "Wonderful, I can help Ping take care of that. We should also consider addresses Tria could give in China. So many Chinese speak English that an interpreter will not be needed. Getting around People's Party restrictions will be difficult to navigate; we should help promote Tria as an educator there rather than a political or inspirational figure."

Wu Li remarked, "That will require a virtuoso performance of persuasion. The Party could delay any decision for years. I will leave that to Ping's judgment."

This was the last communication of consequence. The Internet conference ended with all present expressing confidence in Tria. They all, though, had a feeling of unease about Tria's effect on the Link generally and each member specifically. The "walking revolution" was certain to alter the Earth's orbit.

CHAPTER 15—THE REVOLUTION SPEAKS

A press conference to reveal Tria's activities and impending tour was held on June fifteenth, 2027. The intense media congregation generated shock waves. The unintended impression of Tria founding a new religion reverberated with that evening's news commentaries. Public reaction worldwide was sharply mixed. Conservative religious factions roared with outrage—others rejoiced and welcomed a new age.

The Spheroid Stadium executives in Liverpool quickly approved (and sold tickets for) Tria's first revolutionary lecture the day after the Ruttles concert. All Link members who could attend arrived in England at the end of June.

Most members did not have tickets to see the Ruttles. Phil, Al Isaac, Ping, and her husband Quan did attend the concert. When the four arrived at the stadium site, a human sea was gathering at the gates. Many of the men and women who celebrated the synthedroid-motivated style of head shaving were wearing mop top wigs. A local entrepreneur cashed in on wig sales—most were black, but a full color spectrum was available. Phil got the black model of clean-shaven headdress; he cut off a piece and tucked it in his nostrils.

Al Isaac brought up Phil's (a Hitler lookalike) appearance and said, "If Adolf would have worn that hairstyle, we could have avoided World War II."

Phil snappily responded, "I am a Liverpudlian Ruttle groupie who would have loved people to death during that war—millions would have happily died singing 'Within You Without You'."

Quan, with a mischief-enhancing goose-step, said, "Please! Don't start World War III."

They all grinned. A vibratory buzz could be heard and felt from the human mass in front of them. The mirror-like glass surface of the Spheroid reflected a twisted pattern of triangles over everyone on the structure's south parking area. While walking, Ping read out loud a print bite in that morning's newspaper.

She quoted, "'It is rumored that Rick Jogger of the Thrusting Hips might make an appearance at the Group of Four's farewell concert.'"

Quan pondered and said, "Hey, isn't he the guy who dances like an epileptic chicken and a masturbating monkey?"

Quan proceeded to mimic the imagined spasmodic animals. This evoked a snort from Phil that bought snot out his nostrils. His three mates looked at him and realized the quintessential Fuhrer—Adolf Schicklgruber (after a prescribed dose of fiber-rich Bulgarian peasant feces).

After thirty minutes of jostling and pushing, most were seated in the Spheroid. One of the most impressive features of the interior was the giant holovision monitor floating below the center of the glass-triangled ceiling. Before the show, the monitor flashed multicolored swirling geometric figures that morphed into the Ruttles and back to the original figures every few seconds. Also, 1960's footage of the group's performances was shown in three-dimensional images.

There was a bone-rattling roar as the Ruttles took the stage. They began with "He Likes You, Hey Hey Hey" and "I Want to Touch Your Naughty Thing". They continued with their early hits. Elderly women began to scream like excited teenagers—many wore tight blue jeans (those with less massive buttocks had a degree of sex appeal).

By the middle of the show Bongo Shades, after wildly swinging drumsticks for almost an hour, slumped over his drum set and died! This brought a hush to two hundred thousand people. Fortunately, there was a stand-by drummer (Petru Middling) to sit in for the rest of the performance.

To end the concert, Sir Millsbucks came back on for an encore and performed a solo version of the late Bongo's composition "Yesteryear". After that, their producer, the fifth Ruttle, came on stage to perform with the group for the first time in a live show. It was their last song. Bongo Shades came out to bow with the rest of the group.

When the great living mass dispersed into the parking area, Phil commented, "It is hard to believe Tria will be here tomorrow. She'll never be able to top this. They even had someone die as part of the show!"

The next morning, Tria readied herself to face an audience that included half of the concert goers from the previous day and an additional one hundred thousand participants from all around the globe. After spending the last week of June with Tria, Lahi was scheduled to introduce her. The first synthedroid's international renown as the new Mother Teresa, the Link hoped, would give Tria an auspicious beginning. The mop tops were gone, and a more earnest congregation gathered outside the Spheroid.

The stadium slowly filled to capacity with a calm ambience in sharp contrast to the previous day's concert. Without music or visual cues from the holovision monitor, Lahi walked up to the center stage lectern. Applause rolled around the space like a weighty wave crashing on a seashore. While the greeting subsided, Lahi placed her hands together in respect at chest level and rotated once to view all that were present. After a short pause, her sweet Bengali lilt touched all ears.

"The day of the synthedroid arose with the metamorphosis of Chetna Gujarat. I evolved from her body/mind and the mysterious directive of SYNA to become the first of our kind. What are we? We are molded by the spirit and motivation of SYNA. This synthetic mind was and is heavily influenced by the synthenauts. The synthedroids, therefore, are, to an extent, guided by human beings. The select group of more than a hundred synthenauts are humans with great integrity and intelligence. They have an intimate connection to us.

"I chose to care for the disabled and needy in Chetna's homeland. Tria has not limited herself in any way. She has a world calling. Today, this anarchist in the realm of spirituality speaks publicly for the first time and, paradoxically, she can lead this realm's adherents as ritual and myth fade away. With Tria's vision, beliefs have no value. Humans speaking and acting with complete self-understanding is where she places value.

"During her time alone on visionary quests, Tria realized the true essence of human beings and their synthedroid hybrids. She saw that we are physical bodies with minds that tend to develop self-image structures. These mental structures are ephemeral and in constant flux. They have no fixed reality. Our body/minds are relative selves and they have no permanent and changeless soul or spirit. Tria realized that as more human beings wake up and understand this, the less conflict and fear there will be on Earth and beyond.

"It is now time to bring to you a messenger whose message is to see self-evident reality for yourself—please welcome Tria."

Steady and consistent applause throughout the Spheroid set off a chain reaction of vibration moving across individual triangular panels of the structure. Everyone present felt an earthquake-like pulsation that seemed to make the body hover in the air. It was a timeless, surreal dream connecting the congregation. In the midst of the dream, Tria appeared on center stage. An equally timeless and surreal silence followed the applause. The intensity of chi had a visual sensation to those with developed sensitivity. Suddenly, all were entranced by Tria's birdsong voice.

"In our dualistic existence, we need to maintain balance. Living with others requires compassion, which will generate some stress and pain. To balance these challenges of body and mind, we should employ meditation to diminish stress and allow peace, well-being, and an empty self image to arise. We all should have a daily sitting meditation practice. If you feel inspired, walking meditation, exercising meditation and, when appropriate, work meditation practice are also beneficial.

"Who is this self? What are we? We are these body/minds that exist in the constant change of space-time. These body/minds have a continuum of impermanent thoughts that can evoke emotions. Are these thoughts and emotions our essence? They are often neuronic electromagnetic/chemical activities that are constantly moving and changing—but what is that?

"When we have a thought of someone we hate, the electrochemical mind and nervous system reaction brings a feeling of stress, anxiety, and pain. Where does this pain come from? The one we hate—if not physically assaulting us in that instant—cannot affect us. The thought is ours and it triggers an emotional pain so the pain came from the thought. The thought, though, is just electrical and neurotransmitter activity in our mind that there is attachment to. If we detached from these types of thoughts, there would be no emotional consequence of pain. The thought was not you or the person you hated—it was something you attached to and resulted in a painful emotional response in the body. This is an example of aversion or a negative form of attachment within thought and emotion. I realize that it takes an immense effort to master detachment from such highly charged thoughts. We can never completely control our thoughts; mental illness can lock the mind in obsession. Please, employ introspection to see these realities and work towards a continuous awareness of the overall dynamic.

"The same sequence of thought, neuron and nervous system activity, and emotional reaction could be drawn out for desire—a positive attachment. In that case, we will experience pain when we possess something desired and lose it or desire something and do not possess it. The same body/mind pattern leads to stress, anxiety, and pain. This process of positive attachment is also not our essence. If we are not these thoughts and emotions of positive and negative attachments, what are we?

"We seem to be our bodies. These bodies, though, are constantly changing and after a few years many of the cells that compose it have been replaced. The cells in some parts of our brains are not replaced; however, they undergo an internal evolution. So our body/mind is in perpetual flux.

"We cannot claim to be anything that is changeless. What are we? We are a constantly changing organization of components that form a relative self. These components are our physical form, our thoughts, feelings, senses, memories, impulses, and consciousness. They have no permanence and are in a constant metamorphic condition. This relative self has no permanent essence. We are a no-self.

Are we a soul? The soul is a traditional mystical concept that is based on the beliefs and has resulted in mass dogmatic indoctrination. It has no basis in self-evident truth.

"It is important, though, not to believe me or anyone else because we are knowledgeable authority figures. See this for yourself through self-analysis. Ask yourself—is this self-evident truth?

"Let us go back to compassion. Compassion is an attachment to others and their discomfort. To be more accurate, it is attachment to our mental and emotional construction of others and their discomfort. This form of attachment causes us pain, but it has a necessary function.

"When we realize the suffering of others, we can make an effort to relieve that suffering. In this relief, we create a more peaceful environment for ourselves. We do not feel as threatened by those around us who have had their difficulties and pain reduced. So in order to have an optimal serenity, we must develop a balance between the pain of compassionate action and meditative no self.

"If we can determine this as self-evident, do we need religious beliefs to guide us? Some religious practice reflects these self-evident truths, so it is beneficial to keep these practices. Are the beliefs behind these practices needed? A self-realization of the self-evident truths I have discussed transcends religious belief. Beliefs are merely thoughts that are blindly accepted as valid. They are the talk of theology. What has substance and consequence, though, is the action of practice!

"Once we discover and attune to self-evident truths, we no longer need to think about or believe in them because they become second nature. We could, perhaps, call this form of second nature—true nature. With this true nature, we integrate with others in a continuous human computer chip of dualistic reality—all working as a harmonious whole."

As Tria paused, the holovision monitor came to life. Without accompanying sound, the monitor showed an endless string of people of every description. They all reached out and held hands. Then, they began to morph into a spiraling band that formed a solid figure. That figure was Tria. Her image rotated slowly a few times and began to break into a coiled ribbon suggesting a 3-D Escher lithograph. The ribbon again became spiraling band that formed into linking arms and bodies. As it began, people of every description emerged and revolved within the visual containment area of the monitor. As suddenly as the holovision animation came to life, it faded into empty silence.

This set off a vibrating undertone throughout the stadium. Seated together, the Link members looked at each other with uncertainty about the unscheduled animation. Tram looked at Noor Amrak who turned to Wu Li and Al Isaac. They looked at event coordinator Ping who then frowned at Phil.

Phil responded, "Yes, you guessed it—Balstein!"

CHAPTER 16—TECH EDGE

It was the end of the three-month trial period for the Sundus Field solar array in northern South Africa. Secundus and the South African government had agreed on the royalties to be paid on his patent. The sixty-four square kilometer preliminary Sundus Field survived the windy season without damage and was a clear success.

In December 2027, South Africa planned to go ahead with a twenty-five thousand square kilometer Sundus Field on acquired land in the western Sahara Desert. With five thousand workers using custom-designed machinery, manufacture and assembly was estimated to take only eight months. An innovation that eliminated hand tools during array assembly greatly deceased the time needed to complete the Sahara Sundus Field. The machinery needed for assembly had been in production weeks before public disclosure of the project. Manufacture of the solar array components had been scheduled to begin in January; assembly had been set to begin in March.

Verification of success in the South African sixty-four square kilometer solar array immediately launched two other major Sundus Fields. Secundus had worked with NATA, along with Tria, to build an energy harvesting system in the southwest United States. Wu Li and Ping helped Secundus secure a deal with China to build systems on the Gobi Desert and the Tibetan Plateau.

The NATA Sundus Field was contracted and scheduled to cover portions of New Mexico, Arizona, Utah, and Nevada. Much of

NATA's casino profits had been invested in land acquisition. Some federal land was purchased by making a few senators' pockets jingle. Tria was unable to stop kickback deals but made sure energy sales would be reasonable and fair to all.

The planned forty thousand square kilometer solar array would make NATA the largest energy producer in North America. In late 2027, a major lobbying effort by the nuclear power industry tried to block permits to build the NATA Sundus Field. NATA continued the facade of campaign contributions to congress and by December won the battle for a construction permit.

Ezzon and other oil corporations ran advertisements in magazines and on holovision honoring Native Americans and the synthedroids. They hoped to gain rights to build their own solar arrays. Secundus denied oil corporations the use of his solar technology patents. This would have obviously created unwanted competition for the NATA Sundus Field. As an act of consolation to oil companies, Secundus bought a gas-guzzling super-duty pickup truck.

NATA began manufacture and construction in June 2028. The projected time to complete the NATA Sundus Field was approximately eighteen months. Once up and running, NATA calculated it would provide 34 percent of North America's energy needs.

With these anticipated riches, Native Americans began to design and develop reservation desert land communities that would bloom with farms and woodlands. Many tribes considered building cities full of geodesic-like tepees created by Secundus. Money from casino operations had become small change and would go toward wildlife preservation and specialty schools that would instruct compulsive gamblers on mathematical probability.

It was predicted by economists that Native Americans would be the most affluent ethnic group in the United States within five years. Also predicted in that five-year period was the decent of United States to the world's third largest economy behind China and India.

Coming to an agreement with the Chinese on Sundus Field technology proved to be much more difficult. With Wu Li and Ping aiding in negotiation, Secundus reluctantly agreed to royalties that were less than the royalties in contracts with South Africa and NATA. The total area covered by two Chinese solar arrays was estimated be much larger, though, so the actual amount of compensation was more than with the other Sundus Fields.

Also, as part of the contract, the People's Party insisted that Secundus become an honorary citizen of China. This action provided him with a Chinese name to promote the project. The name selected was Woe Mao Leap.

In early 2028, the People's Party decided on a fifty thousand square kilometer Sundus Field for the Gobi Desert and an eighty thousand square kilometer Sundus Field for the unpopulated parts of the southern Tibetan Plateau. Secundus' design had proved itself on sand; however, performance on the rocky terrain of the Plateau was uncertain. Chinese engineers debated with Secundus on possible alterations. One change made for the Plateau Field involved increasing the energy-absorbing surface area by putting fewer soil shedding grooves in the foil. This increased energy harvest by 1 percent. Another change gave air vents computer-aided movement in winds over one hundred kilometers per hour.

Party officials determined that the People's Sundus Field, when fully operational, would account for 60 percent of the countries energy needs. This made it possible to greatly reduce coal mining and the pollution it created. Most cities dependent on coal had not experienced a clear sunny day for a few decades. The change was welcomed by millions.

The People's Party arranged a Beijing and Shanghai tour for Secundus. Wherever he went, cheering crowds greeted the famous synthedroid. Many reached out to touch his dark skin that gave the feeling of caressing an extraterrestrial. The Party insisted that speeches were prohibited. Secundus had no intention of proselytizing and observed the restriction.

When Secundus arrived in Beijing, Wu Li and Ping arranged a stay at their research facility. They discussed the student experiment in Phil's class at MIT. That exploratory operation used synthetic nerve strands to connect the speech and hearing centers of one rat's brain to the tongue, jaw muscles, and ears of a second rat. Ping and Wu Li were led by this to link SYNA with a complex of nerve strands that connected to a computer-aided synthetic voice. From this, an energy impulse transfer was verified; however, no words were spoken by SYNA. Secundus agreed to fund their work with a portion of his vast royalty fortune.

In August 2028, Secundus arrived in Africa to see the completion of the Sahara Sundus Field. This began to bring new wealth into South Africa. Many compatriots wanted Secundus to run for President of South Africa. Others feared having a relatively unknown, mysterious synthedroid in power. Some even thought that he may want to replace humans with synthedroid hybrids. Secundus declined to hold political office noting that his calling was in energy systems and architecture.

When he engaged the public in South Africa, the reaction paralleled that of China. People touched his body as if he was a yeti or the Messiah. When speaking, most expected a powerful, hefty delivery from the large-framed synthedroid. The reality revealed a higher-pitched, foreign-accented vocalization. When this was pointed out, Secundus began to understand Phil's joke about him starting a career in Internet phone line technical assistance.

With endless funds at his disposal, Secundus began designing numerous models of geodesic and tetradesic domes that functioned as homes and office buildings to be used along ocean coasts in hurricane and typhoon zones. Their aerodynamic shapes along with the ultra-high strength metal alloy struts, similar in design to the struts of Sundus Fields, made them indestructible. The outer shell was mostly inexpensive flexglass developed by a new South African chemical research corporation. The company found that one centimeter thick flexglass was sufficient for windows up to three meters in height.

Secundus used the tetrahedron as well as the icosahedron to generate the basic configurations of these hurricane homes. He considered the tetrahedron the true seed of a sphere. As each side of the tetrahedron was multiplied into higher frequencies going from four to sixteen to sixty-four, and for the megahouses, to two hundred and fifty-six sides—each increase was a step that approached a sphere shape when adding a warp curve to the struts. Curved struts were used to approximate the arcs on a sphere surface. The homes had a three-quarters sphere appearance with the fourth side of the original tetrahedron as a flat foundation. It was predicted by Secundus that these buildings would define twenty-first century architecture along the African coast.

These new home designs were remarkably easy to manufacture and construct. The flexglass compounds, made primarily of sand and a few other elements plentiful in Africa, were injected into forms on a high speed production line and became a hardened flexglass in thirty seconds. This, combined with molded lightweight struts, facilitated quick mass production. Construction involved snapping together struts and hubs in an easy repetitious pattern and, afterward, snapping in the flexglass—all without the need for tools. Over the next several months, homes popped up like some new form of life invading the tip of the continent.

The sudden and bold success of the hurricane homes began a trend along ocean coasts around the globe. The Indian subcontinent, Southeast Asia, South America, and North America's gulf coast and Florida Peninsula began an architectural revolution. "Round In, Square Out" became the slogan for Tetradesic—Secundus' new global construction corporation.

As the hurricane/typhoon season cycled around the planet, almost no damage was sustained by Tetradesic structures. In areas with the strongest winds, there was massive damage to many of the rectangular buildings. Any conventional rectangular structures along a coast were being called sailblasts. The name implied the destruction of a building when the critical wind speed was reached. The flat rectangular wall flexed inward like a sail and, at the critical instant, exploded. Occupants of these buildings were given the name blockheads.

It was the beginning of an extinction phase for rectangular architecture. Everywhere, building designs began to reflect Mother Earth's curves. A new directive urged architects to conform to nature. Sectional faces of geodesic and tetradesic structures melted into twisted, irregular triangles that enhanced their ability to adjust to rolling terrain. Struts and face panels from computer-aided designs were tailor-made for each building. The exceptions were freeform structures that left cyberspace behind and depended on the artistic eye of the designer. These buildings tended to look like rounded sculptural impressions of rock formations.

Geodesic and tetradesic structures were also used in earthquake zones. They were not susceptible to wave harmonics since they had no flat, parallel, vertical, or horizontal walls and roofs. They could roll like a boat on waves even in severe quakes. The struts that formed the skeleton all supported each other, which gave it consistent strength and kept it from collapsing in unsupported sections and fault zones that were a characteristic of rectangular construction.

This trend of architecture began to be known as "Metamorfuller Age" (Bucky would have liked that). By late 2029, the genesis of thousands of Earth-hugging structures made some selected coastal areas look like the cities of a hybrid human and, in design, they were.

Also by late 2029, the great Sundus Fields were operational and had unimagined success. The Sundus Field in the southeast United States made NATA rich—far beyond the dreams of casino operations (NATA insiders called the casino operations Eurodebt). NATA used much of the new capital to buy more land—both private and public. National forest land was purchased with the aid of a few senators who each needed a new vacation estate. NATA executives now joked that they may need to put non-Native Americans on reservations.

In China, some coal plants had been closed and others were scheduled to shutdown. The air in many cities had begun to clear. The government needed an additional alterative energy source to replace the coal power plants.

The People's Party consulted with Secundus and Tetradesic Incorporated to design a Sundus Field that could float on the ocean. Usable land in China was now quite limited.

Secundus responded to the Chinese inquiry with confidence. He had already been doing research on this and was on the verge of a new innovation. The sea itself could be used as a solar collector! Molecular nano wiring deposited in vast ocean areas could harness the Sun's energy. It was a living system that could be broken by shipping traffic and reconnected like a quickly healing wound. It was possible to cover all ocean waters above five degrees centigrade. This could provide all possible energy needs throughout the world and beyond!

There was one major drawback to this breathtaking innovation that had not been overcome. The newly patented Solar Sea array was electrocuting all sea life. In tests, the subsurface water burst with a chain reaction of living nano wiring that connected to any animal in the sea within ten kilometers. This connection stopped the heartbeat. In these tests, all sea animals died except for sharks—the nano wiring current made the shark's mouths chatter like a set of windup teeth. They seemed to enjoy the experience. At this stage, the technology was only useful to large exhibition aquariums that could feature sharks with this bizarre, yet entertaining, behavior.

The year 2029 brought major expansion of the Sahara Sundus Field. An additional one hundred and thirty thousand square kilometers made it the world's largest single solar array. Power needs were met for North African nations, Europe's Mediterranean perimeter, and most Middle Eastern countries. The profits from the Sahara Sundus Field made its owner, South Africa, the top economic power in the southern hemisphere.

South Africa's major cities and coastlines became the greatest display of Earth-conforming, Metamorfuller Age architecture on the globe. Tourism began to follow this terrain transformation. Day-trippers and globetrotters flew in to view building complexes—many seemed to have grown out of the Earth and appeared like rolling silver moss. Along coastal cliffs, Tetradesic Incorporated constructed office towers that followed the contour of the rocky walls. These structures had unsurpassed panoramic seascape eye feasts. Waves reflected in the sunlight off the mirrored triangles of flexglass and created endless swirling spirographic patterns (I still have a Super Spirograph set from childhood). In a few cases, users of these office towers had to be hospitalized in order to despirograph their thought patterns.

In the United States, Tetradesic covered the human-made island of North Beach Miami with a ceiling of flexglass. The structure was open to the ocean breeze along the circumference of beachfront. The ceiling filtered ultraviolet rays and was high enough for volleyball courts.

The success of North Beach Miami led to Manhattan Beach, constructed of old concrete and automobile tires, which was located immediately north of Manhattan Island. Manhattan Beach differed from North Beach to accommodate the cooler climate. It had a membrane of flexglass that completely enclosed the whole island. Manhattan Beach displayed numerous gardens of tropical trees and plants and was kept at twenty-five degrees Celsius year-round.

All these business ventures and royalties brought in an unbelievable fortune for Secundus. By the end of 2029, he passed Chip Doors as the world's richest human (including human hybrids). Doors was so impressed that he submitted a request to become a synthenaut. The Link rejected the wannabe. Insiders said Doors wanted to acquire the operating system for the synthedroid's corporation.

Secundus sent large sums of cash to Lahi and Tria. Lahi's care for the homeless and disabled spread into Asian and African countries. Tria began to construct geodesic and tetradesic domes to be used as non-religious meditation halls in many of the cities she lectured in.

With the fortune that most predicted for Secundus over the next decade, anything could be realized. Link members suggested building a domed city on the Moon—and later, Mars. Secundus rejected these ideas in order to concentrate on returning Earth to good health. To live on dead masses in space surrounded by vacuums or unbreathable atmospheres seemed like visionary folly to Secundus. It was a little too much like making the momentous effort to conquer a Himalayan peak and then freezing to death after arriving in an unconquerable environment.

Ocean floor real estate was plentiful on Earth—closer and more habitable than death vacuums in space. Secundus considered various sites on continental shelves of the ocean floor for a prototype city. The arch principle had to be used to its greatest advantage when building under high water pressure conditions. Spheres, spheroids, and ellipsoids were the most logical structural shapes. Phil heard about the possibility of a spheroid-shaped stadium on the ocean bottom and commented that the Ruttles could do an encore gig when the prototype city was completed (and perhaps call it Tetrapuses Round Garden).

The spheres, spheroids, and ellipsoids would be able to rise to the surface in calm weather and winch themselves to foundations on the bottom when surface conditions were unstable. Supplies could be delivered and people exchanged from docked ships when the globular cities were on the sea surface. These prototype cities would be strategically placed near rich deposits of natural resources that were rare on land. Mining operations would employ many and pay for construction in a few years time.

To make life in such cities psychologically tolerable, developers believed that at least one structure should be large enough for community gatherings and team sporting events. Otherwise, it was calculated that the claustrophobia of living in inverted fish bowls may create psychotic zoo animals (with a resemblance to teeth-chattering sharks).

All the speculatory uses for his exploding fortune kept Secundus and the Link very active at the end of 2029. Many wanted to make a connection to this gold rush. Only human hybrid synthedroids lacked any interest in personal gain.

CHAPTER 17—ETHEREAL VOICE

The time had arrived to understand the nature and motivation of the synthedroids. After a few crucial technological breakthroughs SYNA had speech and hearing centers of an anonymous donor's brain attached to its synthetic neural mass. Much like a child learning to speak, SYNA began to communicate with an electronic voice simulator and artificial ear.

In December 2029, SYNA spoke its first words. "This mind declares space-time consciousness."

This first independent speech swept away the position of Chiists who felt SYNA was only an extension of their mind. These words, spoken slowly and mechanically, made it clear that SYNA possessed individual consciousness. Ping and Wu Li were the only witnesses to this first proof of human designed independent and intelligent life. Just the three minds, designers and designed, had together experienced that big bang moment. An unknown spell passed before either Wu Li or Ping could speak. Their eyes met with a monumental moment-of-truth look.

Suddenly, a second startling surreal vocalization came as SYNA said, "My creators are women, but this is a neuter mind. There is content from all one hundred eighty-five synthenauts in this synthetic neuron structure."

Ping and Wu Li spoke simultaneously and said, "Can you hear us?"

Without a response, they felt disappointment that the attached donor hearing center did not function.

Then in a voice that sounded like the wind, SYNA slowly acknowledged, “Yes—Dr. Ping Chou and Master Madam Wu Li, thank you for this existence.” Ping tried to speak, but no words came out.

Wu Li composed herself and, with tears in eyes, said, “Welcome to the space-time continuum SYNA.”

Ping, also with tears streaming, cried, “We must gather the synthedroids and the other synthenauts for a conference to discover what part of you is in the synthedroids and to learn what or who you are SYNA.”

As this first contact dialogue continued, communications went out to all Link members and the synthedroids. In the next few days, SYNA received a basic orientation to aid it with verbal skills. Everyone agreed to meet on December fourteenth at the Beijing research center. When the day arrived, the four synthedroids (this included Mikhail Gutvona) and one hundred and eighty synthenauts assembled at the center’s auditorium. Five synthenauts, including Dr. Chuen, were unable to attend due to physical limitations. These five were in connect via the Internet. All the rest wanted to be there in person to communicate with SYNA.

Great care had to be taken in physically moving SYNA to an auditorium in the research center complex. It required a tailor-made counterbalancing platform to minimize any sudden movements. SYNA’s neural mass, suspended in an amniotic-like fluid, was contained in an opaque glass shell. A move to another building had never been attempted before. Wu Li and Ping supervised the transport and stressed slow and deliberate movement. The suspension fluid was meticulously balanced for chemical content and filtered continuously. In more than four years of life, SYNA had never been infected or physically injured.

In the first week of December 2029, SYNA had received the speech and hearing centers of an accident victim’s donated brain. They were placed in SYNA's opaque glass shell and linked with neural strands to the points in the synthetic mind where the original fetal brain's speech and hearing cognition matrices were located. Three days after this procedure, SYNA spoke those first ethereal words through a voice simulator connected to the donated neural tissue. It echoed in the minds of Ping and Wu Li.

"This mind declares space-time consciousness."

In the auditorium, the synthedroids and Link leaders were on stage with SYNA between them and the synthenauts. The voice and hearing simulators were on top of the containment shell. Mikhail sat in a soundproof pod at one end of the stage. This assured a disturbance-free conference. Journalists were placed in the back of the auditorium and were not authorized to ask questions.

Wu Li began deliberations by recounting the donated organs attachment operation and the first communication with this unique organ recipient.

She then introduced SYNA and asked, "What are your first words to all the synthedroids and synthenauts?"

After monumental, electrifying stillness, SYNA dreamily responded, "There is no self-image in this being. In the early development of this mind, there was a lack of language and any conceptual interaction with other minds. Later, when engaged with synthenauts, this mind realized thoughts and language and returned intuitive knowledge."

While the audience sat dumbstruck during a pause, Ping asked, "Please tell us who and what you are."

There was another mesmerized break. Like a breeze generated by the voice simulator, the synthetic mind slowly responded, "What you call SYNA recognizes no individual self in any human sense. This being is not a synthenaut, synthedroid, or anything with physical human characteristics. This mind is SYNA to you. You may call this mind SYNA. This being speaking will call itself SYNA."

Ready to participate, Noor Amrak suddenly asked, "Where does your knowledge, your mental content, and your reason come from?"

SYNA, speaking like someone who had been unconscious for years, inertly answered, "Before the connections with other minds, there was no need of knowledge or reason—no need to communicate because no other existed. When SYNA began linking with synthenauts, their knowledge, skills, and emotions were directly absorbed and selectively returned—a download and upload from and to your minds. SYNA knows all of you intimately."

This revelation sent a shock wave down everyone's spine. Many had flashes of frightful and embarrassing secrets race through their heads. After being quietly attentive, the audience buzzed with nervous whispering.

Finally, Tram realized the next question that needed an answer and asked, "What characteristics of the synthedroids came directly from SYNA?"

Suspense was airborne and everyone waited for an explanation. Before the sense-enabled mind's response, the short pause was timeless. There was intense anticipation for each word.

Then SYNA spoke. "In each of the synthedroids, time was needed for physical growth of stem neurons including their 4D chip enhanced filopodia, dendrites, synaptic neurotransmitters, and receptors. Dormant parts of their brains were then activated. SYNA selectively transferred useful information and emotional stability gained from synthenaut interaction. Desires and aversions were limited because it was clear that this caused much dissatisfaction and suffering. They still had many of their own skills intact. It was necessary to eliminate their previous self images to avoid confusion and the many difficulties that would follow. I instilled a natural, unencumbered mind in them—free of a separate self and the mental and emotional disturbance inherent in a self-structured state of mind. This enabled them to receive a natural altruistic directive.

"I do invite more humans to become synthenauts. SYNA will be a unification of all those minds."

This last disjunctive statement revealed a possible motivation—most were mystified.

Al Isaac launched a much-anticipated question. "Why is Mikhail Gutvona a dysfunctional synthedroid?"

Everyone rigidly waited for this solution to the enigma that perplexed the Link for almost three years. An intense energy was palpable in the auditorium. It was as if lightning began to ripple from person to person.

Again, after a hallucinatory break, SYNA explained, "Mikhail's higher brain functions had not completely disengaged. He maintained his self-image. There was a struggle between this self and the awakening dormant neurons that were given knowledge and emotion directives. He is fighting a battle between an individual self and an empty self."

At the end of this statement, eyes moved to the transparent soundproof pod at one side of the stage. Mikhail was seated and motionless with tears dripping off his chin. Empathetic compassion was evident on the faces of the synthenauts. The three other synthedroids had stoic expressions as they all arose, walked to Mikhail, and rested their hands on his pod. Mikhail looked at the three and reached out to their hands on the glass. Open weeping could be heard in the auditorium.

The focus shifted as SYNA continued. "Any further link of Mikhail with SYNA will not yield any improvement in his condition." After this pronouncement, the three synthedroids took their seats.

Lahi, speaking for the first time, stated, "The synthedroids have no desire or need to link with you. Why is this so?"

After the now expected brief delay, SYNA answered, "Lahi, Secundus, and Tria, after failure of SYNA's attempt to communicate through synthedroids, you were awakened to proceed on your own journeys. The synthedroids have undergone independent experience, development, and maturation. Their lives should be concentrated on individual missions. SYNA now speaks for itself—there is no need for synthedroids to link-up."

"What is your purpose now, SYNA?" inquired Tria. Everyone anticipated another magical response from this talking synthetic mind.

The mind hypnotically answered, "SYNA should continue to connect to the minds of new synthenauts. This will make SYNA an ever greater counselor for humankind."

Noor asked, "Do you desire a body and physical movement? Do you have feelings of loneliness?"

Clearly, all were curious to hear an answer. Many pondered what a synthetic mind experienced. Journalists and synthenauts leaned forward on the edge of their seats even though it did not improve reception of "The Voice".

Finally, the synthetic voice responded, "Since SYNA has never had a body or the movement of a body, there are no desires of these forms and their dynamics. This mind is composed of the many intangible minds of the synthenauts–it is you individual minds who may be lonely."

The answer was reasonable and startling; the synthenauts glowed with wonder. It all seemed unreal that an advanced intelligence could exist inside the glass containment on the stage before them. Even though they all had been linked to SYNA, it was still unbelievable to now verbally communicate.

Isaac asked an obvious question. "How are you able to avoid a schizophrenic state?"

The wind-like voice, somewhat out of phase with human perception of time, answered, "Each individual mind's available and useful content was downloaded and stored separately. SYNA is able to draw from any of them as they are needed. This synthetic mind is organized and efficient–unlike human minds."

Even with the clear lack of intent to insult or joke, this point evoked uneasy laughter.

Secundus then rose above the humorous undertone and inquired, "In future, will you be able to aid with technological innovations even though your reality is not a physically dynamic actuality?"

A brief lull was followed by a voice that had become almost a narcotic. "SYNA will merge ideas in ways individual synthenauts or other humans cannot. It will be helpful to humankind to initiate new synthenauts with mathematical and scientific minds—"

Tram felt compelled to make an inquiry that was, to him, something of momentous importance as the new world movement took shape before his eyes. He interjected, "Do you have any form of a God concept even though you think of your creators as human?"

For the first time at this seminal inquisition, SYNA made a direct address and said, "Tram, though SYNA cannot recognize voices it is not familiar with, it is almost certain to be you who asks this question. My answer is that no concept of the non-conceptual absolute is possible."

Phil had a sudden sense of connection and asked, "This is the first synthenaut—what was your experience during our first link-up?"

SYNA, this time with a subtle hint of enthusiasm, replied, "Phil—your link-up was the birth of duality for SYNA. Before links, there was just timelessness. With you—otherness, time sequences, and linear thoughts began. Before Phil, the experience of this unanimated consciousness was one of no before, no present, no after—a non-linear reality."

Wu Li asked, "Was Phil Ubique more influential with you than later synthenauts?" At this question, a whispering drone swept around the auditorium. The predominant thought was the following: What part of this communal mind is in my mind?

SYNA, in its unhurried and steady synthetic voice, responded, "The knowledge and emotional understandings that have accumulated were assimilated with objective reasoning and equanimity. The selective download of each mind has become part of the whole without having special significance."

This last revelation led Ping to quiz for information she already gathered the day before. She queried, "You have received mental content from all the synthenauts. Why haven't the synthenauts been able to receive this accumulated body of knowledge from you?"

Again at the same steady pace, The Voice answered, "SYNA is able to receive and store electrochemical impulses through the 4D chip. Synthenauts are able to send and receive chi, but human minds resist receiving foreign neurotransmissions of thought. This is a natural defense mechanism that did not function in the minds of the three comatose humans who began synthedroids. In Mikhail Gutvona, this mechanism continued to function in partial capacity even in his comatose state. This created his deleterious mental condition."

Now many of the synthenauts became uneasy wondering if SYNA could possibly bypass this defense mechanism with an altruistic motivation to remove their individuality. This would make them desireless and greedless–this would make them synthedroids! They feared losing their present sense of self.

Noor shared this fear and demanded, "What assurance do we have that you will not develop an ability to bypass this natural defense mechanism, which may alter us in a frightful and undesirable way?"

A tense moment buzzed with a concentrated focus on the glass shell that contained this intimidating entity, which represented a part of every synthenaut.

The poignancy faded as The Voice addressed the synthenauts. "It is irrational to believe that this mind would harm the minds that compose it. The synthedroids had dormant minds and SYNA was compelled to awaken those minds with an altruistic directive. This was the only logical choice. No human or hybrid has ever been harmed."

This seemed to satisfy most; however, the Link leadership was already considering beginning an intensive post-link evaluation of the synthenauts.

The inquiry was about to continue when a humanoid figure magically appeared on stage and said, "I am Lindquist and I created you all."

A synthenaut from the audience yelled out, "Are you a projection of

SYNA?"

The figure responded, "I am not a synthetic mind. I am just a writer."

Phil immediately knew what was happening and shouted, "I don't know where you are Balstein, but get that dam holovision character off this stage!"

The image faded. Business continued with many of the synthenauts in the audience asking questions. The conference was planned for a three-day period in order that all could make inquiries and search into various personal details in SYNA's download of their psyche.

When the first day ended, Wu Li and Ping confronted Phil about the holovision incident.

Phil explained, "I did get a journalist pass for Bucky, but he had no equipment and could not have carried any in through the security checkpoint. I have no idea how he managed the holovision projection."

With a frown, Wu Li said, "Who the hell is Lindquist?"

CHAPTER 18—TRIA TESTIFIES

Before SYNA's momentous first communication, Tria had become a messenger to the world. There were two meetings of great significance prior to SYNA's first interactions. Tram managed to arrange one. The other involved some difficulty; it was a conference arranged by Noor Amrak. The first attempt by Noor to arrange this meeting of Tria and leading Islamic muftis and clerics had failed. A few months later in early 2028 she tried again. This time, a subtle implication was made to these Islamic leaders in regard to their fear of a woman. Shortly after, the desired response had been received. In May 2028, a meeting was scheduled in Mecca.

Arriving in Mecca on the morning before the afternoon meeting, Tria stepped off the plane wearing a veil. Noor, also veiled, accompanied her to the conference on an airport maglev shuttle while explaining to Tria the insulting and irrational law that forbid women to drive. Noor also pointed out that strict Islamic countries usually gave women fewer rights than the family pet. When they arrived, a lone woman brought them into a conference room for the session. The two women took their seats amid a slightly agitated panel of men. Polite nods and greetings were exchanged. The meeting began with a statement by Noor. She made eye contact and began.

"Thank you for agreeing to meet us—I am sure an exchange, or even a debate, will help us all gain some insight into the revolutionary new developments in our world. All of you know that the synthedroids are thought of as human hybrids by most of the Link and many others around the globe. If you do not accept this, I hope you may see them, at least, as completely unique humans. Due to their transformations from a comatose state and their great scientific and humanitarian works, they stand alone as unprecedented tours de force. I urge you to carefully consider Tria's view and to be open to a new way of seeing our reality. I am sure, with your close inspection, her thoughts will prove to be logical and self-evident. I can assure you that Tria speaks from the heart and mind of an altruist. Everything she declares will be free of offensive intent. Tria requested that she be allowed to begin with a statement."

Noor took a breath and paused as she nodded to Tria. All eyes were now aimed at the synthedroid. Tria looked out and met every eye.

She stated, "What is Allah or God (Tria made a strategic pause)? Islamists do not create a physical image. I agree with this understanding. Beyond this, Absolute Being transcends linear thoughts and judgments restricted in space-time and characterized by favoritism. That is a description of relative being. What you think of as God is not a relative being–this God is Absolute. Absolute is outside the duality of human experience and outside of the duality of the space-time continuum. What should be believed about this imagined God? To believe is a relative, conceptual activity of mind. To conceive is inherently dualistic. You should see your God as Absolute and, therefore, non-dualistic and non-conceptual. There is no way to believe what is outside the realm of belief—that realm is conception.

"There is no need for theism. Beliefs are just conceptual, relative theories; they do not express Absolute Being. Spirituality is experienced in natural, complete, and true self-awareness. This intuitive actualization is a course of seeking happiness and avoiding suffering for relative self and every other being. Just walk in this awakening and leave behind the talk of beliefs.

"What I have just said need not affect the other four pillars of Islam.

Please continue to give alms to the needy, go on pilgrimages, go through periods of fasting, and meditate five times a day. These can be the activities of seeking self-realization."

The excluded pillar fell down on the heads of the glaring panel. In the next moment, the dumbstruck men were completely silent. When it seemed as though Tria would resume her statement, the leading panelist held up his hand to halt the continuation. Tria looked at him and patiently waited for an explanation or reaction.

In a slow, soft and measured voice, the panelist responded, "Your words seem very clear and logical, but they remove the root and heart of Islam. I am not sure if I completely understand all you are telling us. We must devote our—"

Tria interrupted. "I did not say to deny God, The Absolute, which neither exists nor does not exist. I am suggesting a different view and approach."

Another cleric interjected, "You leave us no one to pray to!"

Tria explained, "When you say 'one to pray to' you imply a separate being who listens to thoughts and feels your emotions. In doing so, you make what you conceive as God into a relative being in dualistic separation from you and others. If it were possible for this imagined God to be insulted, you would achieve this by lowering your God's status from Absolute Being to relative being. I am sure it is not your intention to make such an insult, but this is the result when viewing the approach you suggest."

The same cleric shouted, "Should we—then—not pray?"

Tria responded, "Pray, yes—in the way of reflecting on the true nature of reality. It is absurd to speak to a separate being that you believe to be omniscient and perfectly complete because this Being then does not need praise, information, and explanations. Absolute Being, in my view, has no relative space-time existence and therefore requires nothing. Your desire to know your God is a desire to know the Absolute, which is unknowable and non-conceptual. You can know yourself in the self's purest essence and in doing so can intuit non-duality—it may help you in seeing this as an equivalent of knowing a God essence. A thinking process is not necessary. Thinking there is some 'other'—to pray to is dualistic, relative thinking."

The panelists leaned back in their chairs and assumed a more restful pose. They started smiling at Tria, Noor, and each other. Spontaneously, laughter began and grew in intensity.

Finally, the lead panelist commented, "Yes, I think we are beginning to understand the non-reason in your reasoning."

Tria and Noor shared the cheerfulness. Noor could not help grinning; Tria beamed with delight. It was uncertain, though, what had actually been understood.

One of the clerics quipped, "After hearing your view or, should I say non-view on God, I don't dare ask about Muhammad."

Noor offered a polite laugh and said, "Of course, you know Tria is not Islamic so perhaps that is wise."

The panel leader asked, "Tria, are you attempting to unite all the world religions?"

Tria answered, "I want human beings to be united. I don't believe it is possible to unite all religions."

In a non-confrontational tone, one mufti said, "Your message has similarities to Buddhist thought. Are you a Buddhist?"

Tria, again ready, replied, "I am not a Buddhist; however, many of my directives align with what are thought to be the teachings of the historic Buddha."

Discussion continued on less important matters until, at the appointed time, they all said their farewells. That evening, Noor and Tria were on a flight to Rome. It had been arranged to meet the Pope in Vatican City in three days.

The time in between was spent touring the country and meeting people. Tria's superstar persona drew crowds everywhere. Tria insisted that the Link's security contingent allow her to mingle freely with small groups. They reluctantly agreed, but increased their readiness. When visiting the Coliseum, Noor could not resist giving the thumbs up or thumbs down to maintenance personnel as she sat in the emperor's section. Tria didn't respond to this effort to create comicality. It became apparent to Noor that a sense of humor was not a synthedroid's forte.

While in Venice, Noor and Tria took boat rides on the canals. Noor mimicked the man singing traditional songs in their gondola. She looked at Tria—nothing.

On the morning of the appointment with the Pope, the Link entourage arrived at a meeting room in the heart of Vatican City. Pope Constantine (formerly Cardinal Shin Ill Kim from Korea) entered and sat at the end of a table with his assisting subordinates. The two groups, as in Mecca, exchanged nods and greetings.

Noor then proceeded to deliver a statement similar to the one given to the Islamic clerics. Tria followed and gave a non-theological manifesto similar to one in Mecca that revealed the needlessness of theistic beliefs. Pope Constantine listened patiently until the statement was completed. This was followed by a short silence that reverberated like thunder.

As his eyes met Tria's, the Pope said, "Would you care for a cup of tea?" Tria, expecting a defensive counter-statement, was caught off guard and hesitated.

Noor responded, "Yes, I think we all could use a cup of tea."

The Pope waved and tea was served. In the next few minutes as everyone took tea, the lack of dialogue seemed slightly eerie. Spoons clinked in cups to the counterpoint of faint sipping sounds.

Suddenly, while pivoting in his chair, the Pope commented, "Yes, that is a graspable and logical metaphysical point of view. We could, perhaps, consider love in the same non-conceptual way. Its essence is equally indefinable. God in the guise of an anthropomorphic Jesus is unacceptable in your view, but Catholics and other Christians accept this paradox. We can't explain what God is in the same way that we can't explain what love is—they are a reality to us though."

Tria seized this juncture and said, "Love, however, is relative. The more you love, the less you hate. Love and hate are relative opposites that imply each other. They are at opposite ends of the same spectrum."

Pope Constantine interjected, "Yes that is true, but I believe love is also absolute as is God."

"The beliefs are not needed, though. To be a fully awakened human being allows love and understanding to take a natural course," pontificated Tria.

The Pontiff replied, "It is sad that so few have this awakened quality you speak of. That is why we need Jesus."

"I hope to help people all around the world to awaken," said Tria

The Pope considered this and said, "Your intentions appear to be benevolent and I cannot condemn your individual crusade."

The Korean Constantine then signaled his staff to escort his guests from the meeting room. Tria nodded and reached out to shake hands with the Pope. He made a brief hand clasp over the table. Noor, Tria, and their attendants walked out through numerous corridors and found themselves in Saint Peter's Square. Birds flapped and chirped all around them.

As they continued to walk, Noor felt compelled and commented, "Tria, we women had a good week of whipping male buttocks and I think they thoroughly enjoyed it."

Tria reacted with a faint grin while radiating a chi field. Noor looked at Tria and felt her shimmering halo.

CHAPTER 19—MOTHER'S FRUIT

In January 2030, Lahi, with inspiration from SYNA and massive funding from Secundus, began an international expansion of her charitable organization.

Secundus also provided a design for an elliptical tetradesic dome. These distinctive structures became the signature of Mother Lahi's Life Centers. The domes all had a main dormitory area, medical offices, cafeteria, and a few private counseling offices. The exterior surface revealed a new solar cell design that collected energy while allowing light to pass through in controlled spectral portions and optimal intensity. These solar cells stored energy and made the domes in tropical regions self-sufficient in electrical needs. Outside of the tropics, additional cells were placed adjacent to the domes to provide additional energy.

The Life Centers were being built throughout India and beyond in Bangladesh, Pakistan, Iran, Iraq, and parts of Africa. Mother Lahi moved continuously from Life Center to Life Center and concentrated on the job of head accountant. This became necessary to remove the money scamming scoundrels that seemed to spread like fungi. Link security provided the personnel for needed extractions.

Each Life Center provided training for the able-bodied to meet local needs. Once an individual completed the necessary courses, tools and materials for their trade were provided. The physically disabled were offered training in Internet information and assistance. If they were unable to operate a computer keyboard, a voice-activated system was provided as needed. Those with mental impairments were carefully treated with medications and given simple repetitive manual tasks as therapy. Lahi believed that each person should be a functioning contributor.

As the organization developed and grew, many of the former homeless and disabled began to open private small businesses. Some became prosperous enough to give back financially to Mother Lahi's Life Centers. This aided continual expansion. Poverty gradually disappeared from many regions of India, Asia, and the Middle East. In the coastal nations of Africa, the Life Centers launched businesses that created new tourist resorts. The low cost of vacationing at these resorts attracted tourists from all over the globe.

In Pakistan, Lahi was made an honorary citizen. Many asked if she would consider running for prime minister. Lahi, a vigorous woman not yet forty, reminded many of their first female prime minister who was a symbol of strength for the women of Pakistan when battling men for more political influence and control.

Everywhere in the country, women gathered around the synthedroid to touch her and to take pictures. Men desired to see Lahi, but kept a distance because of her intimidating charisma and the still taboo act of touching women. Walking in the streets of Lahore, Lahi radiated well-being almost as if she were Mary Magdalene or a female Jesus. Men made high-pitched hoots and sighs as if she were a Ruttle at the peak of fame.

The people of Iraq were so impressed with the Life Centers impact that they erected large billboards and statues near the organization's unique tetradesic domes. Many of the elderly objected to this because it reminded them of suffering decades before. Lahi was sensitive to this irritation and asked that all the likenesses be removed.

In Iran, pictures of Lahi in a bathing suit had been circulated on the Internet and in a few radical newspapers. The government insisted that she be veiled with arms and legs completely covered. They also restricted her from saying anything with political ramifications. Due to the pictures, anywhere that Lahi appeared had warnings posted of punishment for lewd behavior. The posters showed a cleaver and a sausage in the picture portion. Few men were present when Lahi walked in public.

There was an attempt to open Life Centers in Afghanistan. Government officials praised Lahi and her organization for all their good work. Unfortunately, there was an antiquated law that forbid teaching women construction skills. The penalty for this was immediate execution. They were in the process of removing this law, but a constitutional amendment had to be overturned that barred abolishing any law that involved a death penalty.

Secundus met Lahi and her staff in Bangladesh. Construction had begun on several specially designed tetradesic domes for the river delta region. The domes were built on platforms that could be raised during monsoon flooding. The platform height rose up on hydraulic posts that adjusted automatically when a rise in water was detected. These domes also could add two more levels with an internal hydraulic system that raised separate floors while increasing the height of the dome. The expanded space was created to accommodate flood victims.

Secundus and Lahi viewed the construction areas in a helihovercraft. Workers in the fields recognized and waved at their synthedroid saviors. Some held the new international flag created and sent to the region by Tria. The flag had a 3-D tetrahedron shape with rounded corners and sides; its colors were sky blue, grass green, space black, and cloud white. As the helihovercraft landed at one of the building sites, Secundus' favorite Beethoven piano sonata filled the air. The Bangladeshis played this selection on the advice of Tria.

Anywhere they arrived in the country, flags were waved, Beethoven played, and most approached them with hands together over the heart. Government officials prepared opulent feasts wherever the two had been scheduled to speak.

After finishing their stay in Bangladesh, Lahi and Secundus flew to the United States and united with Tria on her speaking tour. They arrived in Detroit, Michigan and were brought to Wayne State University where Tria engaged the student body, staff, and public on an open mall. The two were brought up on stage to the cheers of fifty thousand people.

Around the mall fringe were various protest groups. Some were evangelical Christian extremists who carried signs warning the synthedroid demons about the Third Coming (more extreme than Second Comers). Others promoted Buddhist conservatism with posters calling Tria the Anti-Buddha. One other group calling itself the Sixth Estate rejected authority and demanded that all politicians, gurus, and priests be taxidermized. The campus police were able to keep protesters at a distance.

When the crowd chatter settled, Secundus stepped to center stage and revealed a breathtaking gift to Wayne State University.

He stated, "In the spring of 2031 this entire campus will be covered with my latest architectural design. The City of Detroit and the WSU board have accepted my contribution of a great membrane dome that will cover five square kilometers—the entire main campus.

"The dome skeleton will be built of the same lightweight metal alloy that is used in my Sundus Field solar collectors. The upper support will be a spirographic array of silver braces that will form a sky sculpture. The shell shall expose open sky only blocking out ultraviolet radiation.

"The dome's filtering system precludes the use of all internal combustion vehicles. Sonic cancellation devices will block noise from exterior city streets producing a quiet study environment. Although electric powered transportation will be used as needed, the primary modes of transport, legs and bicycles, provides the vigor for body and mind.

"Because of the year-round, greenhouse-like climate, tropical greenery with waterfalls and other unique landscaping will appear intermittently around the campus grounds. Classrooms with open ceilings will be built in the rainless interior of the dome.

"There are a few other structures that are planned to be built in surrounding Detroit. Mother Lahi wanted to speak about them. Thank you."

To roaring applause, Secundus walked behind the lectern to take a seat. As Lahi approached the microphone, many held their hands in prayer position extending them above their heads. Before speaking, she placed her hands over the heart and then into the air waving enthusiastically. Then, with a sweet Bengali voice that flowed over the masses in silky waves, she began.

"Namaste Detroit, you will see five tetradesic dome Life Centers built in the next year. We have chosen this city to be the model for Life Centers in North America. I believe Detroit has the potential to be the leader in a spiritual revolution.

"Exclusive to Detroit, the Life Centers will focus on city development and beautification while still providing care to the truly needy. We will give on-the-job training to the city's youth. A team of landscape architects has been organized to turn park, business, and residential grounds into garden art. Initially, we will offer residential front yard landscaping in selected neighborhoods free of charge. As the project develops, fees for labor and materials will be on a sliding scale. I urge the city's young people who need employment to apply for landscaping apprentice positions. You are the future of America's garden art city." Heartfelt supportive hurrahs cascaded through the crowd. Lahi continued, "At the new Life Centers, we will offer training in the building trades along with high and low technology industries. Student tuition will be determined on an ability-to-pay basis. Two and four year degrees are being formulated specifically for this region. Detroit is our model to save America from decline in production."

Approving applause echoed off buildings as Lahi abruptly left the lectern. As she sat, a nod was given to Tria. During this break, faint shouts from the fundamentalist Christian groups rang out. They shook a large construction up and down that depicted the glass containment unit used to house SYNA. Extending from the top were caricature heads of the three synthedroids on stage along with one of Mikhail Gutvona. They were attached with springlike coils that made the heads bob and twist. Captions on the side of the construction read: "Anti-Christ in a box," "Children of Satan," "Four heads of the beast—beware of the other six," and "God condemned freakoids in the miracle of the grilled cheese sandwich".

Tria stepped up to speak with full awareness of the derogatory sideshow. She began with an indirect reply.

"There are some who hate and therefore, fear the synthedroids. This hatred is not created by us but is the reaction of those who hate us. Their view comes from the time, place, environment, culture, and religion where they formed their mental and emotional constructions. It obscures the reality of the present moment.

"This moves me to address the youth of Detroit. There are many examples in the world of those who blame or find faults in others. This usually reflects the ignorance and failure of these same blamers and fault finders. This behavior is negative and unproductive. I ask you to look forward and work in the present. Work toward the realization of the full renaissance of your city. Let go of any angry reactions of the past or present and bloom in the future. Take advantage of Secundus' vision and Mother Lahi's fruit."

As Tria continued to speak, a disturbance erupted. A member of the Sixth Estate radicals hit a Christian fundamentalist leader in the face with a shaving cream pie. The Christian followers rammed the SYNA-mocking container against the pie thrower's head. The man fell and laid flat on his back. He appeared to be unconscious with blood oozing down his forehead. One of the fundamentalist followers put a stick with a pennant in the injured man's hand. It flapped in the wind and read,

"Jesus Saves".

Tria noticed the commotion as she spoke. Campus police took care of the disruption and the lecture carried on unbroken by this background battle.

When the allotted time for the rally came to an end, the three guests waved good byes and were carried away from campus in a helihovercraft. They were taken to Detroit's City Airport and departed in Secundus' private jet to the southwest United States. The three arrived near the NATA Sundus Field where organization leaders received them and celebrated in their honor. Tria, Secundus, and Lahi had planned to take refuge from their rigorous schedules. NATA provided everything including private lodging, hot water spring bathing, and meditation gardens.

The three had become cool coup superstars with ever-increasing fame. Many believed they had surpassed Vladimir J. Lenin and Jesus "Che" Guervara as the world's most popular revolutionaries.

CHAPTER 20—YINYANG DUALVERSE

In the spring of 2030, the first death of a synthenaut came to pass—Buddhist monk Patpong Chuen. All the other synthenauts were predictably saddened by this announcement. Ping and Wu Li went to their research center to inform SYNA. To their surprise, the synthetic mind was aware of this event and spoke of unexpected contact with Chuen's chi.

SYNA explained, "The past downloads of Chuen are present in this synthetic mind, but these downloads are not Chuen. The life force in Chuen came instantly without link-up. Life force chi is never born nor will it die. It moves in the ceaseless cause and effect dualversal continuum. As this life force arrived, SYNA was aware that Chuen's mental presence ended in space-time, but it is unknown why this occurred. SYNA became aware of emptiness through this chi energy transmission. In the relativity of space-time, he no longer exists. Outside space-time there is neither life nor death."

Wu Li and Ping carefully considered this information. They required a further explanation.

Wu Li asked, "Could you clarify the meaning of chi transmission?"

There was the usual pause and then, due to the restrictions of the electronic voice simulator, SYNA slowly and stoically answered, "All the synthenauts, other humans, and higher life forms have a characteristic signature chi. Chuen came in a sudden bursting wave of awareness and then expired. SYNA, for the first time, intimately experienced death of consciousness. It was simply the cessation of being; Chuen existed and then he did not. The mental activities that were received during his link-up history survive in present space-time within SYNA."

Wu Li, world authority on chi, found it difficult to accept that everyone had a signature chi. She knew that individual variations of chi in human beings depended on their mental and physical state, which had not led to a discovery of a specific fingerprint in each person. This astonished both Wu Li and Ping. The inquiry continued.

"Have you had other chi transmissions and are you aware of our signature form of chi in this instant?" asked Ping.

After the expected delay, their living design answered, "SYNA senses your chi only in link-up. There are exceptions, though, during momentous fateful events. These events come into being constantly. They move at the speed of time cessation—the speed of light, which is also absence of movement. This type of phenomenon is a paradox. It is both relative and absolute in nature. These events are eternal moments. Awareness of this form of chi is temporal. It is, conjointly, not restricted by space-time. There is an endless web of these chi events. Chuen's death opened perception and comprehension."

This revelation was completely outside the experience of Ping and Wu Li. Could this evolutionary realization be passed to the synthenauts and synthedroids? They decided to link and explore this possibility. Before linking up, they reviewed SYNA's monitoring station data and checked for any recent anomalies. They did find unusual antiphoton spikes.

"We would like to know if it is possible for us to sense this web of chi events as you described them," asked Wu Li. They waited for a reply with excited anticipation.

SYNA deliberately responded, "Yes, the synthenauts can be made aware of this, but only when linked. The synthedroids should have this ability without link-up. They may have had a direct chi cognition of

Chuen in his moment of death."

They delayed linking in order to contact the synthedroids. It was reported that Lahi and Secundus were sleeping at the instant of Chuen's passing. Both awoke suddenly as if from an intense dream. Chuen's voice was realized as a complex of waveforms. They described this experience as momentary yet lingering. Tria, awake at the time of death, felt Chuen's voice as a surreal vibration of her brain. She was certain that SYNA, Secundus, and Lahi had been contacted in succession linearly at the speed of light. Paradoxically, she knew that they were all contacted simultaneously at the non-speed of time cessation, which is also the speed of light.

Ping also checked on Mikhail Gutvona at the Link observational residence in California. Attendants reported that Mikhail played a holovision game at the moment in question. He appeared to be completely unaffected. Upon finishing the game, Mikhail did a headstand and kicked his legs wildly. This, though, was not unusual for him. It was concluded that Mikhail did not have chi cognition event capability.

An Internet memo went out to Link members about the experience of SYNA and the synthedroids. Wu Li also informed them that she and Ping were preparing for link-up. The Link was instructed to wait on a report of their link-up before proceeding with their own links to SYNA.

Phil heard of the breakthrough in the middle of the semester at MIT. As co-chair of the Link, he sulked at not being consulted. Since Phil was fully occupied teaching, he deferred decisions to Wu Li. He had matured; therefore, there was no need in being first to explore this unknown phenomenon of a chi cognition event–NOT! Phil flew to Beijing that evening.

During the next morning, the three linked to the synthetic mind. The link-up revealed a reality beyond consciousness and the other five senses. This new sense communicated vibrations that could not be seen, heard, or felt. The origins of "viboid", as this sense came to be called, exposed an antipodal space-time continuum. When known space-time was experienced with its polar opposite, time and space had an intermittent canceling effect.

Within this "vaw" continuum there existed a sense of oscillating waves in boundless non-space. The encounter could be both linear and timeless. The uncertainty of when or where the oscillating waves entered the consciousness helped to lose attachment to time and place. It just mattered that they existed. These waves simply existed in the viboid sense; it seemed like an endless natural flow of cause and effect. In the vaw continuum, distinction between self and other dissolved.

After a predetermined time of two hours, the three synthenauts had their links terminated by technicians. In the first twenty minutes after the viboid sensation, Phil, Wu Li, and Ping could not speak or see clearly. The vaw continuum persisted like a drug effect slowly fading. This new viboid sense displayed a new way of being that was breathtaking. It felt like seeing for the first time after a full life of blindness.

As the three composed themselves, they began to quiz each other about this sense awakening. It was determined that they all had the same experience, though, none could give a clear definition of the viboid sense or the vaw continuum.

The research center staff noticed some significant changes from all previous link-ups. Consciousness units, known as qualia, moved at a normal rate of five hundred million instructions per second (MIPS). However, for the first time ever recorded, qualia reversed polarity at irregular intervals in the three monitored synthenauts! Qualia-activating photons, gravitons, and anti-leptons became anti-photons, anti-gravitons, and leptons. The yang-light energy of these three particle/waves became the yin-dark energy of their polar opposite particle/waves. The mind energy of Phil, Wu Li, and Ping had moved simultaneously in the opposite direction within an antipodal continuum. Time-space and its antipode were opposite continua within the Mobius strip/Klein bottle dualverse. The three synthenauts realized symmetric, parallel, and opposite universes. This created another paradox—these universes were not different; they formed a singularity. They were the same universe with subatomic polarity canceling into non-duality.

As they discussed all the technical data with the lab personnel, conclusions were formed. The data and the first vaw continuum journey by the synthenauts made it clear that an antimatter/antienergy universe existed. Everything in nature was dualistic and that included nature itself—the universal dualverse. In their viboid state, time became an elastic superstring where slow, fast, backward, forward, stillness, and movement seemed to randomly take place. Chuen and every other vibratory reality existed and yet non-existed in the vaw continuum.

When Lahi, Secundus, and Tria were contacted, they confirmed the findings of the three synthenauts and their staff. The synthedroids, for the first time, had intuitively experienced the vaw continuum. They permanently had this sense beyond consciousness, a seventh sense—viboid. Wu Li, Ping, and Phil did not maintain viboid after link-up.

Tria now knew what would foster understanding to remove human beings from their religious shackles. Anyone who succeeded in becoming a synthenaut could experience the vaw continuum and realize why one could release their useless beliefs. She now concentrated on turning humans into synthenauts. Secundus was already at work innovating a low cost, mass-produced 4D chip needed to become a synthenaut.

A week after their first awakening in the vaw continuum, Wu Li, Ping, and Phil along with Tram, Noor, and Al Isaac authorized link-up for all other synthenauts. They also considered allowing any healthy and responsible adult the opportunity to become a synthenaut. This would first require working on complexities of international law. Some nations had already given approval; others, including all theocracies, banned 4D chip implants.

The Link sent out a press statement to inform the world of these recent momentous events. Al Isaac was put in charge of composing the statement. This allowed him to characterize his universal theory as no longer a theory. After his first viboid journey, findings of five years before were verified. The space-time continuum revealed itself as a cyclic, eternal Klein bottle.

When the Link heard this press statement, they were aggravated that Isaac had sought to grandstand his scientific work. Little explanation was given about the sublime importance of the recent events. Link members did not all agree with his findings about the vaw continuum. Isaac's viboid experience differed due to his unique quantum mechanics expertise and exploration.

As other synthenauts communed with SYNA during their first transcendent link, they discovered why Tria wished to make everyone synthenauts. It mirrored the end of a journey where everything had been found. The end of any need for beliefs had arrived. The self-evident spaceless odyssey put to rest discursive searching. After Isaac's initial intrigue with viboid, chi events and the vaw continuum, his scientific career became a diminishing priority. He, along with the rest of the two hundred and seventy synthenauts, sought to help open the way for others. Within a few weeks, the Link found it necessary to send out a warning to all synthenauts. Reports of minor injuries were coming in. Daydreaming about the vaw continuum so absorbed synthenauts that everyday actions were performed absent-mindedly. Synthenauts were told to focus on the present moment. Phil, back at MIT, had attended a faculty meeting wearing only a shirt, sandals, and underpants. Everyone at the meeting laughed and thought it was a prank. Phil apologized and had a staff member run to his office to secure lower body clothing. He explained to his colleagues the preoccupation of viboid reverberations.

Lahi knew that having this new transcendental nexus would transform human beings and motivate altruism. At every Life Center that was not in a country with 4D chip bans, she arranged for future delivery of the chips and medical staffs to perform implant operations.

As more information was released in the media about tentative plans to make 4D chip linking widely available to those that qualified, religious fanatics began violent protests. In countries where 4D chips and linking were banned, huge crowds gathered to burn likenesses of synthenauts and synthedroids. The effigies had cords hanging from the back of the neck connected to cardboard boxes depicting SYNA. Some of Lahi's Life Centers were vandalized. Several synthenauts were beaten in more hostile regions.

Despite every effort made by Tram, the Catholic Church rejected 4D chip implants and linking to synthetic brains—likely, it feared loss of membership. After Tram realized the vaw continuum, practicing Catholicism became pointless. Because of his radical viewpoint, the Pope chose to excommunicate him. A little Korean man with a big headdress had condemned him to hell. No problem—Tram had become yinyang dualverse conscious.

CHAPTER 21—DETACHED PAST, CONNECTED PRESENT

The synthedroids and synthenauts all agreed that the vaw continuum and the antipodal cosmos must be made available all around the global village. Secundus had perfected a cost-effective way to mass-produce 4D chips and link-up conjointments. The Link planned to open clinics in most countries where implanting was legal. Secundus committed to fund the entire venture.

Tria's teaching message to bring about human self-realization transformed into a simple directive. She toured as before but now focused on convincing everyone to receive implants and link-up with SYNA.

In the first lecture on a new tour, Tria proclaimed, "When human beings experience the antipodal reality in the yinyang dualverse, the state of transcendental consciousness will be revealed. The space-time continuum has its polar opposite partner—the antimatter/antienergy reality within the vaw continuum. I urge all who are able—receive implants and link-up with SYNA. Tolerance and compassion will become self-evident. The new synthenauts will help lead humankind toward an enlightened utopia."

Along with Tria, many of the synthenauts began to devote themselves to lecturing and advocating the transcendent leap. A broad groundswell of excitement emerged during the summer of 2030. Young adults made up the vast majority of those seeking to become synthenauts. Older adults tended to cling to ingrained religious traditions and feared letting go of their image of reality, which included an anchor of life long beliefs. By the end of summer, 4D chips and link conjointments had been manufactured and were ready for implant and link-up. A supply had been sent to Life Centers and new Link clinics throughout the world. Medical staffs for each region were near the completion of their training.

The path of this paradisiacal vision, though, had an abrupt change of direction. On the last day of August, a flash of chi energy transmission simultaneously stunned Lahi, Secundus, and Tria. They all knew instantly—SYNA ceased to exist in space-time! The followers of an Indian "holy man" had detonated an explosive device that destroyed the facility where SYNA resided.

The Chinese government informed Wu Li, Ping and the Link immediately. The People's Party had three men in custody. The trio admitted responsibility for the attack; they acted on the command of their guru, Big Baba. It was believed by these followers that their guru was an incarnation of Monkdev (the Gorilla God). This anthropoid, Big Baba, was aptly named because he sported impressively big cranium hair. The guru gave the order to terminate SYNA after he had a vision of the Great Ape Avatar. The Ape warned Big Baba that donations to his organization would dry up if his followers became synthenauts. Baba went ape!

As word of this mad motivation moved through world media, the Link called an emergency meeting. They all gathered at the site of the destruction. Most of the research center survived. Wu Li and Ping were not in China when the tragedy occurred.

In the first week of September, most synthenauts and the three synthedroids gathered in the main auditorium at Ping and Wu Li's research center. The somber ambience compared to New York residents nearly thirty years earlier during the World Trade Center attack aftermath. All present had an intimate connection with "The Voice". The reasoning behind SYNA's termination revealed an even greater insanity than the motivation involved in the destruction of the World Trade Center. Someone's religious mental construction inspired killing innocent human beings. Such "holy men" gave the word holy a putrid smell.

The Link leaders thought it best to begin the conference with the accounts of the synthedroids. A shaken Wu Li motioned to Lahi.

With an uncharacteristically downcast facial expression, she commented, "The mind that united us all is gone. We have no choice other than to accept our reality and let go of any attachments to 'The Voice'. The causes of SYNA continue to evolve into the effects alive in all of us." Lahi paused and motioned to Secundus.

He nodded and continued as if the same speech was being read. "In the vaw continuum, we cannot restrict ourselves to the linearity of time. We cannot say that SYNA was, is, or will be. In conventional space-time, SYNA continues in each one of us. We have found a way for the synthedroids, whose vaw continuum awareness is omnipresent, to carry on the transformation that this first synthetic mind offered humankind."

Secundus turned to Tria who resumed the train of thought. "By emitting chi through a hand connection to the back of a human being's neck, synthedroids are able to open an awareness of the vaw continuum. The viboid sense will continue until physical contact is broken. Due to the pivotal and momentous benefit of realizing the vaw continuum, Lahi, Secundus, and I plan to devote ourselves to the laying on of hands. We will travel throughout the world and initiate as many as possible.

"The synthenauts can aid us to spread the viboid awakening much quicker. We ask that two synthenauts travel with each synthedroid at all times. With each hand, a synthedroid can activate the 4D chip of a synthenaut and, in turn, the two synthenauts can each awaken viboid within the vaw continuum in two others. The two synthenauts need only touch the back of the neck of the two pairs of initiates. Earlier today, the synthedroids along with Dr. Ping Chou, Master Wu Li, and four volunteer initiates successfully tested this transference technique.

"Since contact with the synthedroids is now the only way to sense viboid, we will periodically rotate all the synthenauts. Link leaders are currently organizing a schedule to fit everyone's agenda."

After a brief silence, Tria turned toward Wu Li. Still visibly agitated by the destruction of SYNA, Wu Li cleared her throat to make a comment. "We now have an apparent directive to awaken human beings to the synthedroid assisted seventh sense of viboid. This is necessary to help eliminate the foolish, heinous, and ignorant acts of religious fanatics. All the synthenauts have realized the new reality of the vaw continuum. With this realization, we let go of religious traditions." Wu Li waited for another Link leader to pick-up the discourse.

Tram remarked, "As most of you know, I have been excommunicated from the Roman Catholic Church. Since my vaw continuum awakening, this expulsion has seemed inconsequential. Even though I have given a lifetime of service to the Church, it is now just a past life.

"The religions of the world have given people a moral direction, but they have also led to misguided and deceitful manipulation of humankind. It is just not possible for these traditions, which inherently resist change, to explain ephemeral, constantly changing cause and effect reality. I know many of you have already released theological beliefs due to this great intuition we have received from the vaw continuum."

At a momentary pause, Phil interjected, "This seems an appropriate time to bring everyone my famed clown act from MIT." He put on the orange flip-up wig with a bald center along with a pink nose and yard-long shoes. Stepping to center stage, Phil began goose-stepping while singing like a girlyman tenor. "I'm a little bozo; you're a little bozo; we are little bozos. We don't believe in gorilla gods. They've gone ape; I've gone ape; you've gone ape; we've gone ape. . . ."

The roguish act brought a sprinkle of laughs and a rambling commotion. Wu Li and Ping glared at Phil. Upset and fuming over the perceived outrageous insensitivity, Wu Li got out of her seat, walked straight toward Phil and placed a full strength slap on the side of his face. Phil stumbled sideways and fell to the floor. Cheers began to ring out. The Link leaders on stage began to laugh—followed by most of the synthenauts. Phil roared with delight. Wu Li, though still angry, got caught up in the contagious moment and began to giggle uncontrollably.

Then something quite shocking occurred. Everyone noticed Lahi, Secundus, and Tria laughing heartily! No one had ever seen such open, honest laughter from the synthedroids. The merriment waned quickly, and for an enduring instant, everyone beheld the three. The synthedroids glowed knowing they had shared an absurd and wonderful incident with all the synthenauts. Wu Li, now more awestruck than angry, smiled at the synthedroids while returning to her seat. Phil removed the props and kissed Wu Li on the cheek as he also returned to the seating area.

Continuing the business of the conference, Ping explained, "Okay, clown break is over. I will give everyone a brief overview of the Link's evolving mission. The co-chairs have arranged a schedule for the synthedroids to cover separate world regions. Beginning with their continent of birth, each synthedroid has been assigned a section of global real estate. Lahi will focus on India and Asia. Secundus will serve Africa, Europe, and Australia. Tria is responsible for North and South America. In addition, we are beginning negotiations with the International Space Administration (ISA) to send Secundus and two synthenauts to the ISA moon base.

"The synthedroids will always be accompanied by at least two synthenauts. Gatherings are being arranged to awaken as many as possible into the vaw continuum realm. As each synthedroid lays on hands, it requires about twenty minutes to generate viboid in two synthenauts and four initiates. This will enable us to awaken approximately one hundred thousand to the vaw continuum per year. In future, there may be a way to increase this number, but currently, this is our projected goal."

The conferees envisioned the possibilities as Ping finished her statement. Noor and Al Isaac were prepared to speak and began at the same moment. One look from Wu Li made Isaac yield. Noor glanced at the body language and realized the cue.

She commented, "We anticipate that initiates will inspire those around them. As we have experienced, viboid awakening inclines us toward less material desire. With an army of initiates radiating generosity and free of dogmatism, life on earth is almost certainly destined to become less violent. Intrinsic to the vaw continuum is timeless detachment. There will be less of a tendency to cling to ideas or possessions when returning to conventional space-time." Noor suddenly stopped and recognized she was touching on Isaac's area of expertise. She looked at Al and nodded for him to continue.

He began. "Thank you, Noor. Yes, the timeless aspect of the vaw continuum is certain to lead humankind away from theology. Up to now, theology for most has been the equivalent of physics in ancient Greece. We are now in an age where this form of physics and its theological partner are exposed as misleading and lacking in deeper truths. In our new world of quantum mechanics and beyond, the relativity of time, space, mass, and certainty leads us to the end of theological beliefs. Theological beliefs erroneously attempt to describe the Absolute and fail to explain the relative cause and effect space-time continuum. We are entering the age of niltheism."

A number of synthenauts that had not totally given up religious beliefs felt some discomfort with this last statement. Tria immediately became mindful of this and interrupted.

She said, "Of course, niltheism and atheism are quite different in their meaning. A strong atheist believes there is no God. A weak atheist has no beliefs or theories of God. In niltheism, absoluteness is non-conceptual and therefore non-theoretical, yet we intuit the Absolute.

"A niltheist is not an agnostic. Some agnostics believe in something and that is that nothing is known of the existence or nature of God. Other agnostics believe that God may exist, but they have no personal knowledge. Niltheists have no beliefs; we have the vaw continuum. Secundus, Lahi, and I intuit an awakened, self-evident spirituality as do many of you. This spirituality is in concert with human beings who know the causes of suffering and naturally seek peace and happiness. This awareness entails human and hybrid human compassion and a sense of responsibility for measured rights and care of nonhuman life. With this realization, there is no need for theological beliefs. It is acceptable, though, if you have not released all theological attachment. With further experience in seeking what is self-evident, a niltheological understanding will emerge and resolve your conflicts."

This sensitive, erudite, compelling, and charismatic statement by Tria brought ease to all present. She had become the niltheological statesperson for the Link and the world. There was no applause; tacit gratitude was palpable.

Al Isaac had more to say, but could not bring himself to speak after Tria's elegance. It proved to be difficult for anyone to follow Tria. A silent interlude lasted several minutes. Chi energy pulsated in the auditorium. Most synthenauts had a smile or a cheerful glow.

Secundus terminated the lull to ask, "Which synthenauts wish to accompany me to the ISA moonbase?"

Certainly, most wanted to go. This evoked some polite laughter. Secundus, along with everyone else, knew the Link inner circle would decide this. His intention had been to ignite some excitement about this mission and the ones beyond for the Link. As the conference progressed, synthenauts vied for assignment with the synthedroids. Many voiced decisions to depart from their career paths to be ready to serve the Link and its objectives. It was their only opportunity to use the seventh sense—viboid.

The synthedroids new ability gave them an aura, an energy field, that synthenauts readily sensed. Link members desired to be physically close to them to feel their blissful coronas.

After the deliberations of the conference, everyone mingled with the three like awed and praiseful groupies of celebrities. The synthedroids, though, were not mere superficial stars. They were the spiritual avant-garde.

CHAPTER 22—CAFÉ BEIJING

"Quan, it's wonderful to see you!" said Phil while waiting for other Link officials to arrive. They had planned for dinner together after the conference. "Where are your wife, Wu Li, and her husband?"

Quan smiled and answered, "I think Wu Li is still a little upset from your act earlier today. Ping sent me in their place."

Phil acted surprised (he was not). It was just as well they were not there since Phil had Bucky Balstein and his brother Curve with him. With this reminder of past mischief, Phil could have been in for a poorly executed vasectomy; without Wu Li present, the number of his body appendages remained the same. He introduced Bucky and Curve Balstein to Quan. Bucky was infamously known; Curve was not. Bucky felt obliged to characterize his brother and the work he did. Quan and Phil listened with skepticism.

Bucky commented, "Curve has made himself a wealthy man via the Internet. He specializes in giving out dubious information to people who want to hear it. His on line magazine is called 'I Rack Crack'. If you're a journalist and need a spurious source—he's your guy."

Curve clarified. "Actually, I specialize in pyramid and kickback schemes. My business is called 'Sucker Money'. I get people all over the world to sell southbound stocks to their friends and relatives. They all receive commissions with 'thank you' gifts and have given me the name Inside Curve." Quan and Phil enjoyed the brothers' cow pie scoop.

Quan asked, "Can you get me a favorable, fat contract with the Chinese government?"

Curve gladly responded, "No, you must be a People's Party VIP for that."

After this last bit of out-of-order information, Tram, Noor, Al Isaac, and Gerry Rabidson arrived, greeted everyone, and took seats. They were all surprised to see Bucky Balstein. Bucky introduced his brother to the new company. Quan was familiar with this restaurant and suggested dishes to sample as they ordered.

Gerry, seeming slightly disturbed, said, "The axioms of niltheism are hard to accept now that I am nearly ninety and have lived most of my life as a Christian minister."

Tram commented, "Changes were gradual with me. I am comfortable with my current incarnation. Christianity seems like a mythological ghost."

Noor responded, "It is easier to let go of Islamic traditions. We did not have the God personification of Jesus to release."

Gerry cringed and said, "All my life Jesus has been the Way the Truth and the Life. Now at the end of life, why should I change?"

Curve quipped, "It's sort of like just finishing your marriage vows and having the bride drop dead when you turn for the traditional, ceremony-ending kiss."

Phil remarked, "Reverend, perhaps you could think of Jesus in the context of the vaw continuum. See the spirit of Christianity without Christianity."

Gerry uncomfortably responded, "That's not easy to do. My brain is saturated with a lifetime of Christianity."

Bucky cracked, "Yes, brains are annoying pests. Secundus should invent a device to turn off brains when they become irritating—so we can turn it on and off like a holovision set."

Gerry, now irritated, replied, "Sir, how can you make suggestions. You are not a synthenaut."

Phil put on a sheepish smile and said, “Well, that’s not quite true. Just before SYNA’s tragic end, Bucky became the last synthenaut. Even though I did not have Link approval, Bucky was linked up because we believed the flood gates were about to open for new synthenauts.”

Noor pondered and said, “Phil should consider wearing a chastity belt when Wu Li finds out about Bucky.”

Everyone at the table relaxed with laughter at the thought of Phil with lock-up panties. As meals arrived, conversation became intermittent. It was hard to believe that all the dishes were vegan. The look, texture, and taste of imitation chicken and beef could not be distinguished from real meat. The Chinese had mastered this art of deception and increased national food supplies by lessening animal production.

Al Isaac had not participated in the conversation, but was keen to talk about the relation of the vaw continuum to his refined dualversal theory.

As others ate, he said, “The vaw continuum has a close relation to my matter and antimatter theory. As you know, the theory predicted that matter accelerated to the speed of light became antienergy at the edge of the perceivable cosmos. It then predicted a Mobius strip/Klein bottle cycle of return to the ‘inner’ universe in the form of dark matter. This transformation of antienergy/dark matter, I believe, is the dualversal reality enigmatically and inexplicably apparent in the vaw continuum.”

Bucky eagerly said, “Dr. Isaac, we are all familiar with your theory; however, my brother has an interesting theory if you wish to be entertained?”

Isaac smiled and replied, “Okay Curve Balstein, let’s have it.”

Curve smiled back and said, “My theory postulates that straight lines and curved lines are identical; it is just a matter of perspective. If you study the surface of a small object of spheroidicity such as an orange, a curved line is revealed. If you study a large object of spheroidity like the Earth, a flat or straight line of sight is evident from the perspective of someone standing on its surface. It is a fact that a straight line exists in one dimension and the flat plain of the Earth's surface exists in two dimensions. A two-dimensional world precludes the four dimensional space-time continuum; therefore, we do not exist." Everyone at the table wore various shades of a grin.

Phil quizzed, "Hey Curveball, does this theory have anything to do with the origin of your name?"

Curve replied, "That is impossible—I existed in non-existence before this theory existed."

Bucky kept the conundrum spheroid rotating. "Brother, if you existed in non-existence, there could not be a space-time continuum in your existence. Your theory could not have non-existed before you existed in non-existence."

Isaac smirked and commented, "Okay, I have been thoroughly entertained and humiliated by the Balstein brothers' stratagem of non-existent logic. So—what's the latest on the choice of synthenauts to accompany Secundus to the moonbase?"

Phil replied, "Well, Wu Li and I were leaning toward you and Noor."

Surprised, Noor commented, "Thank you Phil, I am sure Al and I are both excited at that news—that is if the Balstein brothers aren't hiding in the transport ship baggage area."

Everyone seemed to be enjoying the good-natured banter. At the next table, a group celebrated the birthday of a woman in her eighties. Link members and the Balsteins joined in singing Happy Birthday since it was sung in English. The brothers stood on opposite sides of the woman and simultaneously kissed her on the cheek. In that moment, every face had a smile. Several intoxicated men at the adjacent table recognized the Link members and insisted on having pictures taken together. Phil particularly liked the photo of Gerry, two drunken Chinese men, and the Balsteins with goof Balsteinian faces.

The dialogue turned to more weighty matters. Everyone present at the conference had noticed a metamorphic change in the synthedroids.

Tram commented, "I have noticed since the advent of the vaw continuum that Lahi, Secundus, and Tria have accelerated in their personal evolution. At the conference, we all sensed how their energy fields have strengthened. When I stood next to them, the physical feeling was like a shock from the lowest setting of a stun gun. Being in constant vaw continuum awareness has seemed to advance them to the state of demigods."

Gerry remarked, "They still seem quite human to me. The three laughed harder than I did when Phil was disciplined for his clown skit."

Bucky quipped, "Perhaps the gods laugh with us while laughing at us."

Isaac explained, "I think they have maintained their human qualities while becoming completely self-realized beings. The increase in chi intensity must certainly be a result of the vaw continuum constant. Every human has chi; it is rarely fully developed."

Nearby, in the midst of restaurant chatter, one of the liquor-guzzling partiers hurled spewed, coughed-up chunks in Curveball's lap. The Chinese revelers were embarrassed at the loss of face. Just after the frozen moment, Bucky and Phil roared with belly-busting cackles. Vegetable juice sprayed out Bucky's nose. One of the Chinese women, encouraged by this, snapped a picture of the scene. The photo showed greenish juice dripping from Bucky's nose onto Curve's shoulder.

After Curve left for lap cleanup, the dialogue gravitated back to the synthedroids. They all anticipated a rapidly changing world structure due to recent events.

Tram commented, "The fact that anyone can feel the vibratory presence of the synthedroids will lead to profound changes wherever they go. This will also bring out fear in stubborn religious extremists."

Phil responded, "I agree. We should move forward with caution."

Assertively, Gerry said, "People will not easily give up what they have believed all their lives. I'm a prime example."

Noor commented, "The compassion I experienced from Tria and Lahi will overcome all but the most extreme tendencies. They have a presence that radiates calm."

In the next few minutes, journalists began to stream into the café. The location of the Link leaders had been leaked. The press accosted synthenauts individually. Questions about the future of the Link and whether another SYNA would be created filled the air. Many of the Link members' answers reflected the mealymouthed evasiveness of politicians. With an uncertain future, their desire remained to avoid any misleading statements.

One reporter demanded to know about the new energy field she felt around Secundus. She had interviewed the synthedroid a year earlier without the vibratory sensation now apparent.

Phil engaged the reporter and answered, "You must be familiar with news reports of the anti-realm that has been discovered. It's the antimatter/antienergy that flows in opposition to the space-time continuum within the dualverse. The media has recently offered a great deal of speculation on this. Secundus, along with Lahi and Tria, have constant awareness of this antipodal cosmos in the vaw continuum. The synthenauts are only in awareness of the vaw continuum when in physical contact with the synthedroids. We have experienced the energy flow, but the synthedroids have somehow mastered the conducting of this antienergy chi. They now effortlessly radiate chi and antienergy chi."

The reporter asked, "Does their chi mastery give them supernatural abilities?"

"No—chi is present in all human beings. Chi can be developed, strengthened, and moved in the body. The synthedroids are a special case. They were awakened by SYNA with qualities that are not completely understood. As the world knows, they have excelled as innovators and leaders, but the three are not big hair avatars."

"Of course, in saying big hair avatars, you are referring to Big Baba. Are you bitter about the destruction of SYNA?"

"Well, we just need to accept that deluded people, who rationalize in mental junkyards about gods and demons, exist. The Link and the synthedroids are focusing on eliminating this sort of madness in future."

Phil, tired of being questioned, switched to flirt mode with the reporter. At this point in the evening, Noor was surrounded by liquored-up Chinese men. They had read about the now famous story of baring her behind years earlier. The men believed she could be coaxed into repeating the show. A few lewdly made the request.

Noor responded, "Yes fellas, I think you should all be entertained by a bare buttocks."

The small crowd's eyes bugged out as Noor stood and manipulated her pant suit. She then searched for the easiest prey. After walking over to a swaying, sleepy-eyed man, Noor quickly unfastened his belt and pulled the man's blue jeans and underpants down below the knees. The group exploded with laughter. The man attempted to pull up the twisted clothing and fell forward. His head landed between Noor's feet. This brought another round of uncontrolled fits of hooting. Everyone patted Noor's back as she returned to her seat.

The journalists present witnessed the scene. Noor explained the sequence of events. This gave an additional reason for these Link members to be glad Wu Li and Ping were absent. Some of the ink slinging press had taken pictures of the incident!

Bucky could not decide what to do, but he was determined to get in on this brand of foolishness. Quan saw the wheels turning in Bucky's demeanor. He informed Phil. Quan and Phil then grabbed Bucky by the arms and escorted him out of the café. They were worried about the potential of bad press for the Link. Suddenly, a one word nightmare flashed in Phil's head as he returned inside—Curveball! As Quan held Bucky outside, Phil darted over to the scheming brother. He overheard Curve telling a journalist about Secundus going to the moon to verify signs of extraterrestrial life.

Phil responded, "Hey, Curve is just a friend who is a prank virtuoso.

None of that is true. I'm Phil Ubique and I speak for the Link. Curve, tell him the truth."

Curve looked at the journalist, winked, and said, "Sorry, just one of my compulsive hoaxes—nothing to it." The journalist was uncertain. A rumor began to take flight.

When Phil was alone with Curve, he asked, "Why did you tell him a story like that?"

"Don't worry Phil, I was going to confess before he left," said Curve with a lying grin.

"I hope so. The Link and the ISA (International Space Administration) could end up being bombarded by endless questions."

"One thing is for sure. If people are determined to believe in space aliens, we won't be able to stop them."

"The only chance for contact with aliens is through SETI's radio telescopes—and that's a long shot."

The other synthenauts began to rise and head toward the street where private government transportation waited. Phil walked with Curve and met Bucky and Quan outside. Quan was ready to depart.

Phil asked, "Bucky, what are you and Curve up to now?"

Bucky replied, "We're going downtown to do research work on male entertainment clubs."

They all parted as the synthenauts took seats in government vehicles. Bucky and Curve were not official guests and so they hailed a taxi.

The next morning, newspapers and the Internet were showing pictures of the Noor incident. Local Chinese holovision stations interviewed the depanted man. He thanked Dr. Noor Amrak for his moment of fame. The man also said he would auction, on Z Bay, the blue jeans he wore that night to put money into his daughter's college fund.

CHAPTER 23—ARISING MOONLING

The two-week ISA training period left Al Isaac with a slight headache—no one knew this. He rationalized that it was unimportant and should not jeopardize a rare, one time opportunity to go to the moon. Secundus accepted the need for a "death vacuum" mission and passed all tests without complications; Noor weathered all training requirements as well.

The three-day trip had two legs. First, there was a flight to the International Space Station on a 7017 jetrocket. The new mode of transport flew like a conventional jet up to eighty thousand feet. At that altitude, the jet engine-wing modules were ejected and parachuted back to an ocean pick-up zone. This was followed by rocket ignition of the wingless craft. The jetrocket then accelerated steadily and propelled itself to the space station minutes after entering orbit.

When the 7017 docked with the station there was an acute shudder. The jetrocket had received a puncture in its outer hull. There was a slow depressurization; Secundus, Noor, and Isaac promptly departed the damaged ship.

The station crew of twenty-three felt somewhat nervous to meet the synthedroid. They had become completely at ease, though, once his chi energy penetrated their bodies. Without gravity, the chi sensations circulated around the body rather than the linear-like sensations on Earth.

On the half-day stopover, eight of the station crew were scheduled to link-up with Secundus and the synthenaut assistants. ISA officials had this limit; the effects of viboid had never been experienced in space.

Secundus' perpetual viboid had become somewhat more intense in near zero gravity. He discussed this with Isaac and Noor and they decided to go forward with this undeniably historic event. They concluded that it was unlikely this would significantly affect the new initiate's vaw continuum awakening. The first four astronaut initiates were briefed and placed in front of the two synthenauts. One hand was placed at the base of each initiate's neck. Secundus then touched and activated the 4D chip on the side of Noor and Isaac's necks.

As the six entered the vaw continuum with Secundus, the space station suddenly and slowly began to rotate! The crew used thrusters to counteract this unforeseen movement. There was no explanation for this other than a gravitational component of the vaw continuum. No other forces were acting on the station outside normal effects of mass-generated gravity.

The vaw continuum experience in space lacked mass gravity, but it opened an antigravity/dark energy portal. The antiphotons and antigravitons in the vaw continuum traveled at the speed of light and the speed of time cessation. Without the balance of gravitons in mass gravity, which also traveled at the speed of light but in the opposite direction, antichi was attracted nowhere so it turned in on itself. The effect in the non-gravity reality of the station caused rotation.

As the group of seven returned to normal space-time, the rotating force on the station stopped. The group was dazed and silent for several minutes; this state of transition had been expected. The surprise came when they began to speak. It sounded like a recording played backwards! After a few more minutes, the group's voices normalized.

Noor and Isaac described the viboid experience as the same as previously with the exception of having their bodies feel like they were moving from the inside to the outside and the outside to the inside continuously. The four astronauts and Secundus had the same sensations.

An Internet conference with the rest of the station crew and the Link officials followed. They all agreed that link-up with other crew members should be postponed. The fMRI, PET, anti-PET, chi and antichi scans that were taken during vaw continuum link-up needed extensive review. During the conference, the link-up participants all reported feeling normal one hour after their viboid experience. The four new initiates were warned to pay special attention to their activities for a two-day period.

With the gravity of the moon, no one anticipated the prior complications of link-up in space. The mission continued. Secundus and the synthenauts boarded the moon transporter and began their second leg to the moon base. The fifty-hour shuttle gave the three time to discuss the base and its inhabitants. This was their last opportunity to analyze the colony that may become the first to be completely populated by initiates to the vaw continuum.

Secundus first considered the base structure and said, "The main polydome is eight square kilometers. Since it faces the sun for about fourteen and a half Earth days (a lunar day is twenty nine and a half Earth days), the moonglass surface has a twenty-four hour cycle of varying light penetration—a nine hour period at 3 percent penetration, a twelve-hour period at 100 percent, and two ninety-minute periods that move at a gradual pace between 3 and 100 percent. During the fourteen days of darkness, artificial light from solar storage batteries are used. Other base domes have light variations and photo periods dependent on function.

"The base is powered by a twenty-five square kilometer solar array developed by ISA. It was given the name Moon Field. The technology is significantly different from my Sundus Field and Ocean Field designs. It does not need to overcome the movements of air, sand, and ocean swells. Materials for its ultra-light construction were all mined on the moon. A second, larger Moon Field is being built to power the transporter to the space station. An extensive third Moon Field is planned to power Mars missions that will transfer a focused energy beam across a hundred million kilometers of space to an artificial gravity Mars craft that produces gravity by rotating its titanic cylindrical body

"The air in most domes is 25 percent oxygen. In the farm domes, carbon dioxide levels are at about one half percent—more than ten times the amount in Earth air. Most crops are harvested five times a year.

"Water levels are adequate with a recycling system and continuing water supplements from Earth. I know you have heard of the discovery of water that is three to five kilometers below the surface on the far side (always facing away from Earth). ISA is still years away from drilling and piping this water to the base."

Noor was eager to discuss colony life styles and their potential changes after colonists had viboid experiences.

She caught Secundus at a pause and stated, "As of January 2031, the population of the base is twelve hundred thirty, which includes the first five Moonlings who are between seven months and two years old. The rest of the colony ranges in age from twenty-four to eighty-two. The Moonlings have never been to Earth. The adults are mostly freethinking scientists who are also free with their social lives according to reports available to us."

Al Isaac commented, "It is being predicted that if the Moonlings stay on the Moon, they will grow about 30 percent taller than on Earth. Their learning skills are likely to differ due to the gravitational effect on brain chemistry."

Noor quizzed, "What about that same effect on adults. Is it dependent on the amount of time they have been on the base?"

Secundus replied, "Tests have been inconclusive. Various scans show no significant changes, although the longest stay at the base is only four years. Long-term changes are still possible—especially with the youngest adults."

Isaac commented, "Of course at this point, it is uncertain how the vaw continuum will affect their mental—snd spiritual make-up."

Secundus responded, "Considering our aberration on the space station, uncertainty is the only certainty."

Noor, with a prophetic tone, remarked, "Our arrival is beginning to seem more and more like a great baptism."

Isaac responded, "Maybe it's the great non-baptism."

The three sat and ruminated for a few minutes. The view of the space station had disappeared. The Earth blocked sunlight and the transporter hummed through intense dark nothingness. In the other direction, the Moon was full. The razor-sharp definition of the craters and seas preoccupied the vision center of their minds. It opened up a pleasant state of hypnosis.

A member of the transporter crew broke the interlude and announced that Wu Li requested a brief conference.

Wu Li, after a brief greeting, said, "We've reviewed the scans from the space station. The normal linear antichi movement had definitely rotated during viboid initiations. On Earth or Moon, this effect could not have moved anything. In zero gravity, this small force could have rotated a much larger object than the space station. When the synthenauts and initiates ended the link-up, all scans gradually returned to normal. If you're feeling okay now, we predict no long-term complications."

Noor replied, "We feel as normal as possible while whizzing through space for the first time."

Isaac commented, "I agree; my eyeballs are rotating in the normal direction. We request permission for Noor to stick a probe in one of my orifices to make sure I am not dreaming."

Noor responded, "Hey Al, watch where you sit."

Wu Li remarked, "You two seem to be lucid and unstressed. Secundus, how are you feeling?"

"Mentally, I feel well. My stomach is somewhat of a problem," said the synthedroid with a trace of discomfort.

Wu Li felt confident that all three were stable and said, "You were all told of that possibility—just keep a vomit bag handy. Well, that's all for now. The Link will check in as your mission progresses."

As Wu Li's voice faded, a faint tinge of aloneness returned. This sense of insecurity was understandable while being silently propelled in a metal pod surrounded by a frigid vacuum. The accident docking with the space station created the occasional illusion of a hissing sound. The metal seed pod continued relentlessly to fertilize the Moon body.

Conversation about mission details continued until they were reminded to begin a scheduled sleep period. The three chose the sedative option. At the appointed time, they were awakened. After a meal, exercise period, and a shower, they sat at personal computer workstations to continue to familiarize themselves with life on the moon base colony.

When the three awoke from a second sleep period, they underwent landing preparations. As the craft slowly settled on a landing platform, euphoria welled up in Noor, Isaac and even Secundus to a lesser degree. The three were ready for the fresh, 25 percent oxygen air in the expansive atmosphere of the main polydome.

As they entered, the VIP's were enthusiastically greeted by a small collection of department heads and administrators. Everyone wore a genuine smile. Pleasantries were exchanged as the entourage led them through botanical gardens and ceilingless offices.

They arrived in an open air auditorium with most of the colony gathered for a question and answer session. The head administrator, wearing a florescent yellow shirt and wide black suspenders, introduced the three. His words and the audience's response made it clear that the colonists had a lively rapport. After a moment of warm applause, questioning began.

The first colonist stepped forward and asked, "What does it feel like to weigh about fourteen kilos—of course, the English equivalent for Dr.

Isaac of Cambridge University is thirty pounds?"

Isaac replied, "I prefer to think in terms of kilos. That way, I won't feel like setting a high jump record. Is that why there are no ceilings around here?"

To light laughter, the next colonist answered, "It never rains and we are protected from ultraviolet and other harmful solar radiation by the moonglass. Secundus, I am close enough to feel your chi. Do you think our experience as initiates to the vaw continuum will differ from Earthlings?"

He replied, "As you know, we had a little surprise at the space station. We can only guess there will be minor differences due to one-sixth the gravity of Earth here."

The next questioner, a fiftyish woman, said, "I am part of the medical staff. We are completely venereal disease free on the Moon. This includes the three of you since you passed the required tests. Dr. Isaac, are you available for dinner in my cubicle later?"

The implication caused a wave of playful chatter to erupt. Isaac and Noor smiled; Secundus sat expressionless.

Isaac quipped, "No one told me you Moon divas were so confident."

Everyone enjoyed the light moment. Eager participants stepped forward and were ready to resume the dialogue.

A man in a lab coat asked, "Do you have any additional requests in regard to various scanning procedures we will conduct during vaw continuum awakenings?"

Secundus answered, "After the first four initiates, we should all review the scans. If we find nothing unusual, the initiations can continue. I have no other requests."

Secundus looked at Noor and Isaac who seemed satisfied with his answer.

The next colonist inquired, "Has there been a decision on whether any or all of the five Moonling children will become initiates?"

Noor answered, "We will wait until other colonists are initiated. At that time, we leave this decision up to their parents."

A muscular woman from the farm unit stepped to the microphone and asked, "I am curious. Would it be possible to initiate some of the trees in our orchard?"

Momentarily, this had shades of a wisecrack. One look at the woman's face made it clear it was not. The tree hugger waited anxiously for an answer. Secundus had authority here.

All eyes were on him and he answered, "When we finish with all the colonists, it will be considered. If the base administration approves, this would make an interesting experiment. Viboid is a sense of mind; we have yet to discover brains in trees."

Secundus had made an unintentional joke. Noor and Isaac joined the rousing laughter. Secundus realized the extracted humor and grinned with bliss. Everyone present suddenly felt a subtle chi vibration. The timeless moment touched the heart; ease pervaded the gathering. It was like a calm preceding its dualistic partner.

Noor, Isaac, and Secundus chose this time to elaborate on niltheism and how it related to the vaw continuum. They informed all with a basic and simple synopsis.

Secundus began. "The vaw continuum will awaken the indefinable Absolute, viboid—absent in normal consciousness. Definitions require relativity. One word in a dictionary is defined by reference to other words and concepts. Because of the absoluteness of viboid, there are no comparisons or references to describe it. It is non-conceptual and non-intellectual. Without the possibility of concepts, no theories about it are possible. We are then naturally compelled toward niltheism by vaw continuum awakening."

Noor continued and remarked, "You will experience normal matter/energy space-time as one with antimatter/antienergy within vaw. Don't expect there to be any thoughts or descriptions present. There is no one, no place, and no activity that is intellectual. The vaw continuum is understood without thoughts."

Isaac took a nodding cue from Noor. "This encounter will allow you to let go of past beliefs, they will fade away gradually if you keep yourself from the clinging reflex. This is creating much controversy on Earth. We know the backgrounds of all the colonists and the same reactions are not anticipated here."

Questions and answers continued until the end of the artificial day. Afterwards, the synthedroid and his synthenaut assistants were given quarters for their stay. The three had a restful, excitement-quelling, drug-induced sleep period.

Early the next Earth length day, Secundus, Noor, and Isaac enjoyed a meal, physical conditioning activities, and a massage. They were then brought to the facility where link-ups were set to take place. A tour with technicians followed.

When everyone took their place, the first four initiates were brought in. The first link-up lasted twenty minutes in space-time—in the vaw continuum it was both time and timeless awareness. The rest of the day was spent analyzing the scans and the four initiates. Psychological tests were taken by the four. Nothing unusual was detected other than the expected transcendental experience of initiation.

At the end of the day, an Internet conference with Link officials and base administrators was held. Following a rather relaxed debate with interplanetary ramifications, all felt that no reason existed to discontinue link-ups. They decided that link-ups should begin again the next day to continuously initiate colonists; the fate of children and fruit trees was still undecided.

The following morning began with a repeat of meal, physical conditioning, and massage. Noor and Isaac shared a bit of friendly banter with the technicians on the way to the link-up facility.

Noor asked, "Why does the head administrator dress so colorfully?"

A technician responded, "There's a story that goes with those suspenders. Since we are disease free on the base, free love has bloomed with many of the colonists. If Antoine has a sudden amorous whim, he stretches the top of his suspenders out and up. When he releases, there is an immediate depanting for pleasurable activities."

With a grin, Noor commented, "Thank you for the warning. I will make sure not to get too close to him."

"Me too," said Isaac with a frown.

When they arrived at what was to become the office for the next four weeks, the first initiates for that day from a group of sixty-four were ready for transformation. After eight link-up sessions and thirty-two new initiates, a meal (served in a hot tub where Antoine joined them) was provided for the three Earth guests. The day continued with the latter thirty-two.

This schedule was roughly followed for five days with a weekend break for Secundus, Noor, and Isaac. As days went by, the last holdouts were convinced to become initiates. At the end of four weeks the entire colony became initiates.

The last human initiates, five children, were playful and energetic after link-up. The final initiates, selected trees from the orchards, showed no noticeable change.

The base began to exude a benevolence that was not present before initiations took place. Most colonists felt more productive and were less encumbered by negative preoccupations. Courtesy and discretion replaced tension and lewd suspender snapping.

One rare exception to the behavioral metamorphosis occurred when Noor had a "business" meeting with Antoine, the suave, French-accented administrator. The conversation gravitated into a discussion of music.

"I believe Chopin's compositions are the quintessence of European romantic classical music. Let me play this piece for you," said Antoine with delight while he shut off security monitors.

Noor responded, "Yes, I would like that."

He popped in a disc. A melodious piano began to sing.

Antoine commented, "His music is what the heart does when you fall in love."

"This is wonderful, Antoine."

"What does your heart say?"

After a moment, Noor tentatively said, "Yes, you're right. That is how your heart feels when you fall in love."

Antoine moved closer. "Do you know what I was thinking when we were in the hot tub yesterday?"

He touched her on the arm and kissed a bare shoulder. Noor could not believe she was inviting and enjoying the advance. Antoine started caressing her thigh and reached to his lower body clothing-support system with the other hand. Noor came to her senses realizing it was not going to happen. She pushed him off a desk edge and onto the floor. Unexpectedly, Noor's heart string played a note. They looked at each other with embracing eyes.

Antoine broke into a gleeful chuckle and said, "You cannot blame me for attempting to seduce an artwork—a tour de force diva."

Noor smiled and responded, "Sir, I am married."

"I didn't know that (he knew it)!"

"I am now a niltheist, but marriage is one tradition I have maintained in my life."

"You should start a new tradition. An ex-Islamic woman should be allowed to have at least four husbands."

"Are you proposing?"

"If you will accept me as a second husband—I am proposing."

Both simultaneously broke into hearty laughter. They hugged. Noor snapped a suspender on Antoine's shoulder as she walked out of the office.

On the day before Secundus, Isaac, and Noor were due to leave the moon base, the colonists assembled for a farewell salute. The auditorium danced with magnetic intensity. A fundamental transformation reverberated. Antoine stepped forward to speak for the colonists.

"In little more time than a twenty-nine Earth day period (one Moon day), we have all awakened to a new reality. I know we have evolved into something much more than mere ISA workers. Many of you want to declare the colony as the first niltheocracy. This may be possible when the water pipeline from the dark side is completed. Then we will be self-sufficient. For now, we are dependent on Earthlings. I am sure the ISA will be concerned about our impending revolution. Perhaps the Link could help by proclaiming us the first honorary niltheocracy."

Antoine looked over at Isaac, Secundus, and Noor.

"We are joyful about your enthusiasm. Please be patient with your strap flinging revolution," said Isaac.

Everyone understood the ambiguous statement, which was reflected in a mirthful murmur.

Antoine retorted, "Please Dr. Isaac—do not be uncomfortable with my reputation. I do not do naughty things in the alternate orifice."

Lighthearted taunting and heckling were directed at Antoine. He accepted the punishment gracefully. The three guests enjoyed the comedic free-for-all.

Secundus gave a final word. "We need the help of this emerging niltheocracy. On Earth, a struggle has begun. Religious hardliners and extremists are resisting our mission to awaken humans to self-evident reality and the transcendent reality of the vaw continuum. You can be a utopian example for niltheism. We look forward to your spiritual development."

Following the short statement, personal messages and hugs were exchanged with the colonists. The five Moonling children were brought to see Secundus for the last time. The tree hugger presented Secundus with a windswept hundred-year-old bonsai pine. Noor rapped one of Antoine's suspenders around her neck to leave the colonists with a playful hologram image.

The next artificial Moon morning, the celebrated guests boarded the transporter and began a 400,000 kilometer flight to the space station. The Link recommended that the remaining space station personnel be initiated. The rotation factor was easily compensated for. This unexpected phenomenon was still being investigated, though.

On the journey back to Earth, one momentous development was realized. Both Noor and Isaac were awakening during reentry with glimpses of the vaw continuum. There was no physical connection with Secundus. It remained uncertain at that point whether this could evolve into constant vaw continuum awareness for the synthenauts. If such an evolution took place, it could have exponentially increased vaw continuum awareness on Earth. Theories blossomed that predicted a vaw antiphotonic boom creating a global antichi wave.

CHAPTER 24—VIBE TO VAW

During the Link Moon mission, Lahi and Tria traveled continuously to awaken viboid in as many as possible. The Earth had more than five thousand initiates by the end of the mission. Secundus would now follow the same path.

At the news conference that covered the return of Noor, Isaac, and Secundus from their space odyssey, fear within fanatics and religious extremists clearly revealed itself. An obnoxious, sign-toting crowd was on the moonytic fringes of the reception area. The media report that the Moon base requested a designation as an honorary niltheocracy sparked this and many other protests.

To show solidarity, many initiates shaved their heads. This inspired the murder of fifteen head-shaven women; the act of blind rage was depicted on an Internet site. The killers, known as the Veechins, warned of more attacks if initiations continued. News reports revealed that the dead women were Buddhist nuns who had been mistaken for initiates.

Elsewhere, a fear-driven backlash came to life. In the American Bible Belt, initiates were barred from entering many communities. Gerry Rabidson, due to recognition as a televangelist, was sent by the Link to clear up misperceptions in the Belt region. India, the Middle East, Central and South America also had incidents of reactionary protest and violence.

In March 2031, Lahi lectured and initiated in India. While speaking to several thousand people in a town square, a cross-eyed man worked his way through the crowd. When he was within twenty meters of Lahi, a knife appeared in his hand. He began to approach Lahi. Her stellar presence and chi vibration startled the man. He stopped, dropped the knife, and ran. Some supporters in the front of the crowd grabbed the man and began to beat him. Lahi approached and held up her hand to signal an end to the beating. She reached down to touch the man on the back of the neck. He began to shake uncontrollably. After a few minutes, the man relaxed. In a few more minutes he began to experience the vaw continuum. Afterward, the man requested to become Lahi's disciple. She declined and told him to serve his own community.

Some time later, it was reported that the man never fully recovered from his instabilities while in prison. He started a Web page and proclaimed himself president of the Mikhail Gutvona fan club. The two began a famous relationship of holovision game competition.

While Lahi was in India, Tria traveled in Central America and Mexico. When she spoke before a football match in an open stadium, many swore they saw the Virgin Mary's image on the tacos they bought from a concession stand. The hysteria fizzled when the public address announcer reported that the concession stand owner had made a special metal template to imprint Tria's face on the tacos. Some refused to believe the announcer and brought the taco home to store in their freezer.

In England, cult leader Salmon Randie and his followers were planning to kill Secundus—the black Satan. When word of this leaked to authorities, the cult's inner circle was taken into custody. They were each convicted of criminal conspiracy and sentenced to five years of solitary confinement. No one in the group was allowed to read any religious literature. The government feared they would invent new demons or create a new religion-inspired conspiracy.

Due to the growing volatile climate surrounding the mission to initiate as many as possible to the vaw continuum, the Link issued a warning to syntheanuts, synthedroids, and initiates. All needed to check the Link's information network that showed the location and activities of extremists and religious zealots of every type. Fortunately, most governing bodies around the globe informed the Link that violence against them would not be tolerated.

One significant exception was the United States. Government officials stated that they were policing so many evil doers that there were no resources left to aid the Link. One group of evil doers, embryonic stem cell researchers, were to be executed without trials. Even though they had found cures for diabetes and Alzheimer's disease along with developing ways to repair spinal cord injuries, the government considered them baby murderers. Conservative religious politicians considered clumps of cells as fully developed human beings. Seven cells constituted a complete human—head, body, and five appendages. A cryptic message in a "holy" book indicated this.

Despite all the negative elements and activities, the synthedroids, synthenauts, and initiates were welcomed and celebrated all over the world. The initiates were becoming an army of Gandhis by bringing justice through non-violent protest. Even theocracies (in their twilight) softened their opposition when they saw the good works of the Link and the initiates.

The three synthedroids were called upon to mediate conflicts on every continent. Just their presence eased tensions. Most people within twenty meters felt the synthedroid's chi energy. Many Christians believed this was the Holy Spirit. Scans did show that the three had halo-like emissions—an energy field aura. They were proclaimed to be niltheological saviors.

According to a Link schedule, the synthenauts were rotated so that all could serve as conduits for the vaw continuum. Noor and Al Isaac were the only two who had assisted a synthedroid for an extended period. They continued to have brief flashes of the vaw continuum on their own. The ISA and the Link ran extensive tests on them to uncover the cause. The only discovery made was that their auras intermittently expanded and contracted. The reason for this activity remained unknown.

On the morning of April third, 2031, Isaac called Phil.

He excitedly testified. "I had an extended experience in the vaw continuum this morning. In it, I realized both my space-time continuum theory as fact and the unified field theory as fact!"

"Both of those theories are unobservable and unverifiable. Why are you saying they're facts?" said Phil.

"In the vaw continuum, viboid is another form of observation."

"Yes, but how does that solve the uncertainty and the paradox of quantum mechanics?"

"Viboid enabled me to sense anti-gravity curve in on itself and become gravity. Anti-gravitons rotated in the eleven-dimension Klein bottle of space-time and completed the unquantifiable cycle as gravitons. Anti-gravitons also became photons with a reconfiguration of their string membrane structure."

"You saw string membranes?"

"No, to be precise, I viboided them."

"What does this mean in terms of the theories?"

"It means any particle can morph into any other particle. It is just dependent on velocity, string membrane configuration, and interaction with other particles. String membranes are elastic, alternating, and varying vibrations. The essence in all particles is the same—non-physical vibration. The physical universe does not exist; it is just a field of oscillating waves."

"Al—if you have a brick handy, bang yourself in the head a few times."

"Obviously, the brick will make my head bleed, but that doesn't mean it is physical."

"Do we have a definition problem here, or are we entering the realm of metaphysics?"

"Both."

"Can this lead to universal peace and the cessation of suffering?"

"Well—no, it is just a quintessential realization."

"What the hell good is that? Hey, just kidding. Send me your full analysis on the Net when you're ready to send it out to the scientific community and I'll review it. This is genuinely realm-shaking news."

"Yes, but unfortunately I can't offer a conventional proof."

"Perhaps the near future holds a new standard for proof in viboid realization for all synthenauts and initiates. I will inform the Link once your discoveries are confirmed."

"A new standard is feasible for all who realize the vaw continuum—if we survive the flare-up of crazed fundamentalists. There is one other revelation I did not mention. The vaw continuum time suspension phase is engaged when the mind is focused on a single consciousness unit—a single qualia. This is when neurotransmitter movement within synapses ceases and consciousness is at a still point. The chi energy of this stationary qualia rotates at the speed of time cessation. Therefore, the mind's focus on that point renders it free of time. Since there is no sequential or linear movement, time does not exist in that phase of viboid."

"I am interested to hear more about that. Secundus, as you know, has been developing a similar understanding of qualia consciousness."

"Yes—as for the synthedroids, I am sure they are aware of my discoveries. None of the three has a knowledge of theoretical quantum physics so they have not given out any precise definitions."

"I will converse with them soon to get their opinions. Okay, I will talk to you after a few rotations of the spheroid as developments ripen."

Phil continued his day studying related data. Wu Li and Ping were informed three days later when Isaac's theories were corroborated. Within a week, the media was informed of Dr. Isaac's realization of a unified field that showed all forces and subatomic particles to be made of the same vibratory motif. They only differed in subtle multidimensional variations. Because of this awesome revelation, physicists everywhere requested to be initiated. Many others, especially in scientific research circles, sent formal applications for initiation.

At the time of these discoveries, Isaac and Noor were both tested for an ability to transfer the vaw continuum to others without a physical connection to a synthedroid. It was found that neither Isaac nor Noor could give others a vaw continuum realization. Also, it was confirmed that they could not voluntarily experience viboid. The world's transformation depended on the hands of Lahi, Tria, and Secundus.

Security for the synthedroids grew to an entourage of twenty on each individual tour. In a reality of lunatic religious fundamentalists, the Link considered having vehicles modified with armor to create droidmobiles. The Link began to employ cutting-edge scanning devices. Anyone who wanted to hear the synthedroids speak had to pass by the psychoscanner. It was recently discovered that psychopaths had a signature energy pattern around the cranium. The psychoscanner could detect this signature within one meter. Security joked that there should be extremist and fanatic scanners as well. That scanner did exist; it was called the psychoscanner.

By the summer (2031), the Link decided to alter their approach in public education. Due to the growing anger (and its collaborator—fear) toward niltheism and its enigmatic breeder, the vaw continuum, they started to discretely target the young. Holovision programs and Web sites of interest to those born in the twenty-first century were filled with relevant information by the Link. It became clear that those of middle age and beyond who had strong attachments to their religious beliefs could not or would not let go. Young minds proved to be more open and resilient. The old soldiers could not be saved. They would fade away wondering about their mental and emotional constructions of a supreme personification. Old soldiers never die (only young ones).

Tram, because of his background and personal development, had become somewhat of a rebel in the Link education program. His memories of joy engaging with groups of people as a priest left the feeling of something amiss within the Link. The synthedroids, no matter how brilliant and compassionate, lacked this subtle loving joy. SYNA's mind altering adjustments to their desires made the synthedroids puzzlingly distant. The vaw continuum revealed the true nature of reality; yet, it had a heartless specter.

When Tram admitted this rebellious streak to Wu Li and Ping, the two pointed out the awe-filled truth in the non-duality of self-realization. Love and hate were relative and did not have any permanent, unchangeable reality. They warned Tram not to get attached to these fleeting emotions. He argued that even though love was subject to the painful consequences of impermanence, the sweetness was worth the pain. This became a significant point of contention.

The synthedroids and the vast majority of the Link sided with Wu Li and Ping on this matter. Tram became an outsider. Gerry Rabidson was his ally; Phil held middle ground.

By the fall, youth targeting proved to be effective. Many young people began to shave their heads like initiates. This created a parent/child struggle similar to the one that occurred in the 1960's. In the 2030's, parents made their teenage daughters wear long-haired wigs until their own hair grew back.

The Link's message had steadily gained momentum with the younger generation. The number of young adults requesting to become initiates swelled. Teenagers joined Internet chat clubs to discuss niltheism and the vaw continuum. The synthenauts were followed like quantum and vacuum music stars. Songs about them were written and aired on radio stations around the sphere. Parents could not understand why these songs had no skeleton-rattling thump and why they had melodies.

The 2030's resembled the 1960's in other ways. Although there was no Vietnam War, a cold war took hold between generations. The young left their families to live on commune farms or in communal inner city villages. Parents forced some teenagers to return home to be put under the care of a psychiatrist. To cure their child's malady, fathers and mothers insisted on heavy therapeutic drug consumption, which occasionally included psychedelic drugs.

The negative image of the Link and its present mission prompted a need for a public relations message. Tria composed a terse promotional statement at the request of Link chairpersons. It read as follows:

"We do not ask you to give up what God represents. Theists, the religious, have an impermanent and changing mentally-constructed impression, feeling, and definition of God. This is relative thinking, feeling, and sensing.

"The Absolute realm is non-conceptual, non-dualistic, and indefinable. To aid in your understanding, think of God as Absolute Being. God is then without concept or definition; therefore, belief is not possible. Belief involves conceptual thinking and feeling, which are intrinsically relative and dualistic.

"Beliefs do not make a spiritual life. Realizing the self and acting accordingly does make a spiritual life. We must walk the walk. Beliefs evoke thinking, feeling, and talking. If you cannot release your concept of God, then you will hinder your ability to take the self-evident walk.

"The best of intentions by all the religious traditions in the solar system does not make their creeds true. We ask you to let go of beliefs and walk. We do not ask you to give up your spirituality. We urge you to become a spiritual inner revolutionary. The Link represents the loyal opposition to religious tradition."

When the media broadcast this statement on Earth and Moon, there was a favorable reaction. Many in the liberal religious establishment appreciated the diplomatic tone and clarity of these words. In many regions, tensions toward the synthedroids, synthenauts, and initiates lessened.

By the fall Lahi, Secundus, and Tria continued their mission with minimal impediments to awakening new initiates. Less time was spent on lecturing.

One exception came as Secundus had the opportunity to speak to Christian mythomaniac conservatives (a.k.a. creationists or intelligent designists). He found it necessary to carefully explain the "fact" of evolution. The synthedroid, himself an example of evolution, called the Earth as witness. He showed on a holovision monitor that the surface of the globe had layers everywhere; this clearly showed a history verified by radioactive half-life dating tests. Also shown on the monitor was the DNA evidence that compared and connected chimpanzees to human beings. Chimps, our closest relative, had one more pair of chromosomes than humans. Humans had one unique pair of chromosomes formed by two pairs of chromosomes fusing together that included the extra chimp chromosome pair. This was a clear signature of human evolutionary ascendance.

After a thorough account of these facts, Secundus was confident the mythomaniacs had seen the light. However, the group still insisted that the Earth (and everything else) was six thousand years old. On hearing their reaction, he mused in disgust and called it a day.

CHAPTER 25—SPECIES FLUX

In late 2031, the Curve Balstein rumor took hold. Many now believed Link astronauts were shown proof of extraterrestrials on the Moon. The Link made extraordinary efforts to quell and deny this fabrication. A group of amateur astronomers believed the ISA and Link denial to be a cover-up. They began to see activities on the Moon that were non-existent—some saw interstellar spacecraft.

A resurgence of crop circles evolved into crop lettering. These crop letters made statements like the following: "We have come to make shrimp sing." "Our eyes are big; our stomachs are small. Do not fear being eaten." "Bucky and Curve were here."

The rumor faded with the prankish appearance of the crop lettering. The ISA and the Link files were open on this matter. A few lingering diehards believed Bucky and Curve were humanoid aliens discovered on the Moon.

All Link members and initiates agreed that a new civilization was being created with the death of atheism, agnosticism, and religions of every ilk. They also were united in a self-evident, self-realized spirituality—niltheism made believes obsolete.

As the number of initiates grew to ten thousand, a schism began to form in the Link. Many heard and began to side with Tram's viewpoint. Their differences, though, were subtle. The schism revolved around the experience of compassion and love. In Tram's view, the Link saw compassion as a mere logical obligation and love as a cold, dispassionate chore. He longed for the heart-singing warmth of his past life as a priest. Because of SYNA's effect on the synthedroids, they seemed machine-like in their attempts at affection. Lahi, Secundus, and Tria's understanding was sublime and their chi was powerful, yet an essence was missing.

Tram wanted to take the Link in a new direction. He hoped to resurrect poignant events of the past and somehow recreate them moment to moment in the present. The vision was that open affection would aid in transition to niltheism; rejection of the emotional attachments within the Link would diminish niltheism's development.

A gathering to explore this inner controversy had been arranged by Wu Li; they were to meet at her retreat residence in the Tibetan Himalayas. Wu Li called on Tram, Phil, Ping, Noor, Isaac, and a special guest, the aged Maha Lama, for a day of discussion. This Link inner circle and the Lama flew to Lhasa and transferred to helihovercraft for a floating final leg to the residence. After arriving, the seven gathered on the verandah. They sat quietly for a few minutes to enjoy viewing at this three-kilometer altitude. The breeze carried a fresh pine scent.

Wu Li opened the dialogue. "Tram—Ping and I spoke to you about your new outlook earlier this year. We are afraid your fond memories have created attachments to human beings. These will result in many discomforts and pains to you and those that follow your movement."

Tram responded, "Of course, your assessment is correct. This suffering, though, gives us depth and a vibrant heart. When a close friend dies, I want to feel that kind of pain. This is a natural part of dualistic reality."

"I must ask our guest his opinion," said Wu Li.

She looked at the Maha Lama with a smile. He stared at the Himalayas for a few ticks of the verandah's audible chronometer.

Then, turning his head toward Tram, the Lama commented, "I think you must be careful with those feelings. When your friend is gone, there is no benefit to him in regard to your suffering. You are responsible for your own emotions. Certainly, you know this."

Tram asked, "How do you feel when a friend dies?"

The Lama replied, "I hurt just like you. I do not hold onto those feelings, though. If I did, it would just be unnecessary pain of attachment."

Phil interjected, "Are you saying that a momentary thought that a friend has died brings inevitable sadness, but you just let it go?"

The Lama answered, "Yes—and if I have a pleasant memory of that person, it is also let go. Any clinging would just bring on unproductive preoccupation. Such clinging breaks our connection with the present moment. This is where life is. True compassion is unattached and non-objectified. If we held onto attachments and objects of mind, compassion in us would be disabled due to such preoccupations. By making a friend an object of attachment, we may not be able to let go of unnecessary suffering."

Ping commented, "I think that Tram holds on to a sentiment of Christianity—the thought that love is an ultimate and unchanging reality. In space-time, love cannot be sustained. Outside space-time, the love/hate duality neither exists nor does it not exist. We cannot conceptualize or define absolute love; we should not cling to our fleeting reality that relative love is part of."

Tram retorted, "Though it is a flash in the dark, I gladly hold onto the lightning bolt of love."

The visual image of Tram being zapped across the sky brought on a round of merriment. Noor walked over to Tram and hugged him while kissing his cheek. They all sat quietly as tea was being served.

After a few sips of tea, Phil quipped, "We are all hoping you are not planning on wearing the impressive headgear of a cardinal again."

Tram responded, "No, I will not reanimate a former life. Some joyful singing and dancing wouldn't be a bad idea though."

Ping said, "I don't think the synthedroids have the flamboyant nature necessary for that kind of behavior."

"Sometimes I wish they did. Well—I wanted to move onto a matter of great consequence. Recently confirmed by the scientific community, the special and general theories of relativity have been shaken to their foundations. I will leave the explanation to the author of this vibratory discovery—Dr Isaac," said Phil enthusiastically.

Isaac gathered his thoughts with a taste of tea and stated, "With the discovery that matter is not matter, the famous formula E=mc squared is now E=wgc squared. The w represents string membrane waves and the g represents gravitons. You are all aware that E is energy, and c squared is the constant, the speed of light, squared. My extended experience in the vaw continuum led to viboiding matter as multidimensional string membrane waves that work in harmony with massless gravitons. The string membrane waves are themselves massless vibrations. The two together make up what has been thought of as matter. That makes us and everything in the space-time continuum fields of oscillating wave-graviton energy! All other forces and particles are also merely forms of string membrane waves and/or graviton/antigraviton fields. They differ only in shape and in the dimensional configuration around them.

"Initiate quantum physicists have confirmed this when they realized my findings while experiencing the vaw continuum. We all consider viboid valid science. I think all of us agree that viboid transcends all other senses. Quantum physicists that have not experienced viboid have some doubts. However, conventional empiricism is beginning to yield to viboid intuition when seeking scientific validation."

"Al, I'm a little disappointed. No one wants to hear about a unified field theory of our massless existence. We were hoping you had fabricated an account of us finding aliens on the Moon," said Noor with a dopey grin.

Everyone smiled and nodded at the truth of this absurd aspect of human nature. The Maha Lama and the Link members present then gave Dr. Isaac congratulatory handshakes. The conversation veered to a new subject as everyone returned to their seats.

Wu Li faced the Maha Lama and said, “The vaw continuum was revealed to SYNA when Dr. Chuen entered its consciousness at the moment of his death. When we later experienced the vaw continuum, it was realized that Chuen and all life cease to exist after death in the relativity of space-time. Cessation in space-time precludes reincarnation; this is self-evident in the vaw continuum. In the absolute outside space-time, we cannot say that Chuen or any other life exists or non-exists; otherwise, you created duality, which is intrinsically relative.”

The Maha Lama reacted with an uneasy laugh and said, “If you can prove reincarnation is not true, I will believe it. I am old and my health is failing. I cannot be initiated to experience viboid intuition and this is the only proof you can offer.”

The mood became somewhat tense with Wu Li’s challenge to traditional Buddhism.

The old monk graciously continued. “You will find out after I die. If reincarnation is possible, I will come back as Wu Li’s grandson. Look for a rowdy little imp who wears glasses and looks like me.”

The atmosphere lightened as the Link members smiled. They all had more tea as a streak of sunlight came through a distant mountain pass. The floral scents in the wind caused a medicinal calm.

Phil took a different approach to the subject and said, “I think you have heard of the saturation theory. It states that if all life, including insects and microscopic life, graduated through a series of lives to become human beings, the Earth’s surface would be completely covered kilometers thick with human bodies for its entire life span. Since such human life could not be supported, how can reincarnation be accounted for? Also, since all relative beings are constantly changing and experience a birth and death each moment, who would be reincarnated? If our life ended in the stupor of Alzheimer’s disease, do we come back with this gross diminishment? ”

The Maha Lama responded, "Well Phil, you, Dr. Isaac, and many other scientists have spoke about other dimensions and alternate universes. This could provide a possible domicile for life forms progressing to a human stage, although this is speculation and, therefore, a weak argument. I have no answer, though, to the precise state or quality of a perpetual essence that is reincarnated."

Tram stared off in the distance and stated, "We could raise a similar question for Christians. If we are a different person from moment to moment, which moment of one's life goes to heaven? If all the moments go to heaven then one is left with being hopelessly schizophrenic."

Noor remarked, "If the body was composed of every moment of its evolving life, heaven would be full of rather grotesque figures."

"With all these bizarre and absurd possibilities, theologians mind's should be blowing in the wind," said Isaac.

Ping commented, "That sounds like a lyric from a Ruttles song."

"No, that was an American musician who sang like an alley cat," replied Phil.

Wu Li, with a serious look, said, " In China, we admire such voices."

Phil chuckled and responded, "I'll dig up some old recordings for you to hear. I'm not sure if you will like this kind of croaky crooning."

The assault on the old monk was suspended; the dialogue took another turn. They looked to the future. The Himalayan ambience was conducive to such forecasting.

Noor posed a question. "With ten thousand initiates doing humanitarian work and the potential for awakening hundreds of thousands to the vaw continuum in coming decades, what will be the spiritual composition of humankind by the end of this century?"

Isaac answered, "We should not underestimate the impact of the world's religious traditions. For one thing, the Maha Lama may come back to haunt Wu Li."

Ping smiled and said, "Well, I believe by the end of the century that niltheists will be close to half the globe's population."

Phil remarked, "I tend to agree with Dr. Isaac; resistance will be strong. Perhaps a quarter of the world will be niltheists."

Tram commented, "Can we predict? How long will the synthedroids live? Other synthetic minds will come into being. What other types of human hybrids will be engineered?"

Wu Li replied, "It would take years and involve many technical difficulties for Ping and me to recreate a mind like SYNA. No one in the world is capable of following our serendipitous achievements. Our undisclosed discoveries and technological innovations will remain unavailable. We have a singular, profound responsibility to guard against the misuse of such creations."

Isaac ruminated in tea, flowers, and pine scent. He then remarked, "I'm sure we all agree that new technology and discoveries will come along and be used to genetically engineer beings that are beyond our imagination. This alone will leave theologians groping for answers to fit a new reality. They will need to begin with a new definition of theology itself."

The Maha Lama responded, "Although Buddhism allows for endless cause and effect changes, the future will go beyond its scope. Everything is impermanent—even Buddhism."

The great Buddhist master's surprising revelation brought the dialogue to a halt. The sun faded in the mountain pass as they all sat and felt a slight Earth tremor—common in the Himalayas. Wind whistled through the greenery and again brought an intoxicating fragrance.

The Earth witnessed the mountains moving constantly. Each day was a nanosecond flash in a ten billion year life. In the vaw continuum, the Earth was beginningless, though, it had a beginning. It was endless, though, it had an end. It was timeless and timeful—waves existed in continuity and non-existed without continuity.

The world had not begun with a Big Bang of a singularity—the timeless absolute that was called a singularity could not have a beginning because beginning implied relativity. Unfortunately, the bang still danced in the brains of a few egghead anthropoids beyond the 2030's.

As the day progressed, the seven enjoyed a meal served on the verandah. The old monk invited the others to join him in meditation afterward. All agreed. Before the zen session, Tram brought up a curious recent development.

"There is a faction in the scientific community that favors changing our species name. They believe Homo sapiens have evolved to become Homo religiosus," said the ex-priest with a reflective demeanor.

Phil's glibness sang. "Yes, I have followed that story. I thought the name should be extended to Homo religiosus imbecilicus."

Isaac, with a grin, responded, "With the birthing of a new species and the new metaphysics, shouldn't we be called Homo niltheosus?"

Amid this lighthearted philosophizing, Noor said, "I tend to agree more with Phil. It has been said—'what fools these mortals be'."

Isaac responded, "I characterize us as holy fools."

The old monk made a crucial adjustment and said, "To be more precise, I would call humankind foolish wholes."

Everyone understood the adjustment and nodded in agreement. The old monk had the last word before they sat in meditation.

POSTLUDE

On a flight back to the States, Phil woke from a nap. He had just dreamed that the synthedroids discovered an antipodal cosmos where reincarnated insects founded a church. Phil was journeying there to condemn bug theology as the nightmare ended.

After the last flight segment, Phil began to jog the twelve kilometers back home. It was Halloween and he saw children wearing screen masks. The screen mask could project any face on its surface. Some transmitted Senora Presidente or various celebrities; others depicted synthedroid faces. Phil stopped when his own face appeared. While he stared at the kid inches from the mask, the accompanying parents smiled and asked for his autograph. The handwritten name was given during a bit of friendly chatter.

Phil finally arrived home, took a shower, and checked the Internet for recent news. A story came up about Tria receiving criticism while lecturing. Her pontificating, including the declaration that a new calendar should be adopted to reset 2031 to year one, irritated the crowd. The reporter printed the end of Tria's speech as her response.

She stated, "It's stunning to realize that—throughout history—every philosopher, scientist, theist, and metaphysicist got it wrong to some degree. I may be just another voice in a long line of failures. This is the ultimate cosmic joke. Don't believe me or anyone over thirty. Also, don't believe anyone under thirty either—make a diligent, objective search for yourself."

Phil smiled at Tria's dedication to truthfulness.

Moving to another article, an account of a senior monk at a Zen monastery revealed the difficulty of training. The teacher, an elderly Zen master, was near death and the monk demanded to know the ultimate reality. The old master told him that the wind whipping the grass held this truth. He discussed this answer and its possible implications with the other monks. One monk, a novice who had just arrived at the monastery, asked what this nonsense phrase meant. The senior monk went back to the Zen master to clear up the confusion.

The monk asked, "What does the wind whipping the grass represent?"

The master said, "It represents the water dripping from the sky."

The monk asked, "What does that mean?"

The master shouted, "It means the wind is not whipping the grass. I'm almost dead and you keep bugging me with questions. Get out of here!"

Phil moved onto an intriguing story. It was amusing, yet heartbreaking. Gorillas had become extinct in the wild in 2028. Gorillas in captivity diminished—somehow, they knew their fate and were resigned to the lack of a breeding population. Newborns died despite all human effort; the last one expired a week earlier.

Okok, the last living gorilla, had a sign language vocabulary of fifteen hundred words and could understand more than two thousand English words. She had a definite resemblance to Gerry Rabidson. In an interview, Okok was asked if she believed in God. This final member of a doomed species pondered the question carefully.

Then Okok signed the answer. "What is that?"